REVELATIONS

REVELATIONS

BORIS CHRONICLES™ BOOK THREE

PAUL C. MIDDLETON

MICHAEL ANDERLE

DISRUPTIVE IMAGINATION

LMBPN Publishing
PMB 196, 2540 South Maryland Pkwy
Las Vegas, NV 89109

First US edition, 2016
Version 1.05, January 2021
Print ISBN: 978-1-64202-990-1

CHAPTER ONE

NVG Research Base, Russia

Zakhar was worried. The concern he felt hovered like a dark cloud over his head, shadowing his days. It had been months since there had been any contact with his boss, Konrad. He had been warned that the movement would soon take steps to gain more influence over the government, necessitating this base going dark.

By now he had expected personal contact or communications from Konrad or one of his lieutenants. The lack of any interaction with his commander made him feel like he was standing in the eye of a storm, waiting for disaster to strike.

All communications were to be initiated from outside the base. Even with no incoming calls, he followed the communication protocols Konrad had ordered.

Zakhar believed that the Russian government didn't appear to have a clue that his base existed which showed their growing incompetence. If true, the political structure would be ripe for eventual takeover. That Konrad had kept the project secret confirmed that he was a worthy leader, at least to Zakhar.

Despite the nagging worry about the absence of contact, he was more concerned by what some of the teams had found. They had confirmed the existence of an unknown alloy at the opening of the main cave mouth, although none of his scientists had figured out how to replicate it.

Damn it.

The metal seemed to be from out of this world, quite literally. With the news reports the base still occasionally received, Konrad and the NVG would need every possible advantage against the damned Americans and, in particular, the corporation that was releasing all this new technology.

The reports from the investigation of the cave system worried him and he admitted he spent a fair amount of his time thinking about it.

He had no idea how Konrad had found the caves and was honestly unsure if he wanted to know. Mapping the caverns with radar and sonar had failed, and their manual progress was too damned slow. The teams were losing people. They simply disappeared. These losses were scattered and not linked to any single mapped offshoot tunnel.

As typical in an underground cavern system, the earth made many strange noises. Some of the noises from the cave might be natural rumbles, rocks falling loose from erosion or slight changes and vibrations from the explorations.

Nevertheless, the men swore they had heard sounds which they described as wheezing, roaring bellows from some sort of creature. The cries were so low pitched that not all of his men could hear them, but each time people had mentioned the sound, one of his team members had disappeared. The unexplained loss of people in the tunnels was causing huge morale problems.

No blood, no sign of rock fall, no weapons fire heard, the impact on the teams was worse than if there was a visible battle. The people were just gone. So far the count was low enough he could blame it on inexperience and lack of attention. He had even explained their disappearance by saying that missing personnel had gotten lost by going deeper than ordered.

Zakhar didn't believe that.

Trying to think ahead, he ordered defenses to be constructed facing the cave entryway, but that was against specific orders. He certainly did not want to aggravate Konrad, so he did not dare do anything too radical.

He'd started sending down teams with no less than three people. Now, Zakhar's problem was an entire team of three was missing. Similar to radar, radios were unreliable in the caves, so his teams were hampered in their rescue efforts. The group of three was only six hours overdue, but he had a bad feeling this time.

Zakhar rubbed his face, looked at the clock and sighed. He said a quick prayer, not sure why since he didn't go to church and gave the order for all remaining teams to pull back for the night.

The groups searching for the missing had been down there for a total of eighteen hours between their own shift and now the added search efforts.

Certainly, they would start making mistakes in what

could be a deadly situation even if there wasn't something down there hunting them.

Zakhar wasn't one to believe in aliens or the supernatural. At times he would admit Konrad had enough weirdness that he thought him vaguely alien. But, Zakhar finally decided to put it down to the man's driven personality.

Now? Now Zakhar wasn't so sure.

The local legend that told of a devil trapped in this very region by Saint Michael was becoming more believable every day. After these incidents and dealing with Konrad, Zakhar wasn't sure where his core beliefs ended anymore.

He wasn't sure if he should be more worried about something from inside the caves or the attacks that had been taking place on NVG convoys. Zakhar almost wished this operation had government sanction at least. Then, if something really went wrong, he could call in the army.

Instead, if the military found out about what they were doing here, then he and all his men were probably going to get a reprimand at the end of an AK-74. The Russian government would not like the idea of potential alien tech on their land being recovered and researched without their sanction.

Zakhar pursed his lips and finally nodded his head.

He would have the ramp into the cave system dismantled and replaced by a lift. His engineers could rig something quickly.

If there was a creature stuck in the caves, Zakhar would not be responsible for releasing it into Mother Russia. He believed his government was corrupt and ineffective.

However, he loved his fellow countrymen.

The Beast was angry.

When she had encountered the first two creatures, she thought that they had fallen into her realm. Once she had realized, from their taste, rather than their looks or smell, that they were human, she was confused.

She had not encountered a human in these caves since that odd and powerful one had thrown her into the caves and blocked the entrance. Although she had searched extensively, no other reachable exit was discovered. The Beast felt a growing need to look again after encountering the first human thing. After all, they had managed to find their way *in* somehow…why not see if out was an option?

Then she had encountered a group of three of these strange humans. They were invading her space… her territory… her world!

This wouldn't be allowed. She was the Queen of her area and nothing was going to change this.

The Beast followed their scents and found herself in a cave that she knew well. There was an opening that the Beast had tried to use to leave these horrible caves long ago. Before she had accepted this area as its territory. The overhang on the wall at the lip of the exit had defeated all her attempts to escape.

Now, the invaders had built a ramp.

A ramp, unlike any the Beast had thought humans capable of making, was there. It was made of metal, and lead easily up to the exit of the cave. The Beast realized she could leave. All she had to do was scare these strangers out of her home.

Make them fear *her*.

The Beast didn't want to kill them unless they attacked her first. For all she knew, the powerful, strange man was still watching, waiting.

Patience was a construct of time and time was a meaningless concept for one who had experiences like she had survived.

The Beast approached the ramp, letting out a bellow of anger at their trespass. The ones inside the cave dropped what they were doing and fled in terror up the ramp. It sauntered after them, pleased with the result, moving slowly enough to allow them to escape. Having no way to know what they were doing ahead of her, the Beast cautiously climbed the ramp to the exit.

Reaching the top of the rise, she had found herself breathing forest-scented air for the first time in ages. She paused, drawing the air deep into her lungs, experiencing the long-missed smell with a kind of rapture. That short stop had left her in the open, exposed. The rapturous interlude had blinded the Beast, leaving her oblivious to others of the strangers' kind approaching until the cracking, stinging annoyance of their weapons broke its reverie.

The Beast roared her anger and defiance at them. The short, sharp pains kept coming as the long metal sticks continued to bark. Realizing that the stings must be coming from those flares and cracks, she sprang forward, moving at a speed those with the poles could not, and did not anticipate, from a creature of her size.

Rage had taken it. Anyone holding one of the stinging poles became a target of that anger. Some were gutted by the Beast's claws, others had limbs sheared cleanly in a single bite. A few kept firing, trying to hit the Beast as it fell upon their comrades. Unable to anticipate the movements and speed of the creature, most of their shots missed, or hit those same comrades.

The few that struck the Beast did it no real harm.

Many of the remaining attackers threw away their arms and fled. But they were marked by the weapons they carried with a scent that The Beast could track… It would hunt them down until its rage was satisfied. Those who fled to the houses it ignored - It would have time to decide about them later.

CHAPTER TWO

Wilderness near Archangelsk, Russia.

"Well that took longer than you promised," Boris said with a smile to Janna.

"It's not my fault that the damned site had spoofing measures in place to disguise where the Etheric energy was being drawn." Janna retorted. "And Konrad had hidden the location well. Probably only a handful of his top people knew where this place was. All the convoys headed here stayed. At least four hundred people - could be as many as eight hundred," she grumped.

Boris scratched his cheek, "Yes, I know. And we picked up some interesting local legends for the area. It seemed odd that the belief in the fight between Michael and the Devil happened west of Archangelsk, but narrowing down where they changed from 'the battle was to the west' to 'the battle was to the east' was a stroke of genius. Not something I would have thought of," he responded.

Janna considered his comment, "I wouldn't have thought of it either until it became obvious something screwed the ability to triangulate based on whatever it is drawing on the Etheric."

Boris looked around, "Now if we just knew what those whispers we're both hearing are, I would be pleased."

Paul spoke up, putting down the binoculars he was using to observe the camp. "Does that base seem to be, I dunno, a little quiet for four hundred plus people being there? I mean I'm not seeing *ANY* movement."

Boris lifted his binoculars and looked through them. It was daytime, and there was no evidence of anyone moving between the timber buildings. With the snow that wasn't so strange, he thought. That there was only a handful of buildings that had snow properly packed against the outside, with smoke emitting from their chimneys. Those would definitely be occupied.

There was also a cleared area around that particular cluster of dwellings. With the heavy layer of snow, it was impossible to tell if that had been part of the original plan or if structures had been knocked down to clear it.

As a paramilitary base either was plausible.

"Okay, we go down and investigate," Boris replied. He looked at Janna and Alecta. "You two hang back. There is definitely something odd about this whole situation.

If it weren't smack bang in the middle of the area Janna had designated from their research into local legends, Boris would have been disinclined to investigate. But they had also found a man in one of the local hospitals who had been brought in, with an NVG patch on his gear. The man had been found about a hundred kilometers away, with one of his legs sheared off at mid thigh and delirious from a wound infection.

He'd kept ranting a string of numbers that the doctors had blamed on his delirium. But the interesting thing to Janna was that they were exact GPS locations for this encampment. It was well disguised, each of the houses partially dug in, and probably had camouflage netting over it during the warmer months.

It wasn't likely an area where satellites would often look either.

So, they'd come into range in the command container during a snowstorm after every other attempt to find this base had come up empty. It seemed that sometimes, no matter your support, luck was still needed to make progress.

If the fifteen agents that agreed to help them hadn't run down those legends for her, she'd have been in trouble with someone. She wasn't sure who. And that theory had been based on a flimsy note that Konrad had written on a report regarding possible alien technology referencing Michael and The Devil. They still needed to find this last base. There were too many records for it to be disinformation, and taking out a paramilitary group was like excising cancer. You didn't chance leaving some cells around so it could regrow.

Janna had decided to research it. The reference had triggered a memory about legends in the Archangelsk region. Her delving deeper had paid off. They could have spent weeks searching the area if Anton hadn't found that patient and gotten what he'd been saying out of the medical reports. Boris was just glad that the small hospital didn't use electronic records. Otherwise, the Government might have beaten them here.

He hated to think how long it had taken Konrad to find the location. Actually, that wasn't true. The thought of how much more frustrating finding the location would have been for Konrad was amusing. If Boris had been frustrated for over two months trying to find the place after Konrad, it had to have taken Konrad even longer.

They walked down into the camp, staying in the open. There was a nervous tension in the air. Boris had felt its like before. Whoever was holed up in those buildings was full of fear. It could be easily smelled as they got closer. "Don't make any sudden moves. Something has these people downright terrified."

As they approached the building, they heard the distinctive sound of a machine gun being charged. Boris held up his hand and yelled "Ho. We mean you no harm!"

There was silence, but no guns fired. "May we seek shelter? We got lost hunting and could use some better shelter than a hole in a hill."

Still silence. "Ah well, if there is no other option I guess we'll have to seek refuge in that cave on the hill."

"No. Come up. Anything but handing the Beast more people." A gravelly voice, worn with worry yelled back. Boris looked at the others and nodded. They walked up to the house the voice came from, and the door opened. As they walked in Boris saw a pistol and several rifles trained on them, in the hands of obviously nervous and twitchy individuals.

The gravelly voice, clearly male, spoke, "Who are you really? It's coming into full winter. No one hunts this far north in the winter. Just because we won't feed the Beast, doesn't mean we won't kill you."

Boris took less than a second to make the decision. He moved at his fastest speed, grabbed the pistol from the closest person pointing at him, disarming the person without the pistol firing.

Then, he used them as a human shield and yelled. "Put down your weapons. You have no cause to aim at us. We, however, have plenty of reason to wipe this entire encampment off the planet." Boris tossed the pistol towards his group and pointed at the patch on the captive's arm.

Moving his arms, he was surprised to find it was a woman he was holding. Damned cold screwed up his sense of smell too much.

There had been a few women amongst the NVG they'd killed or captured, but not many. And several of those they'd *caught* had been more like rescues.

He nodded to those aiming at him and his voice became more of a growl, "We've been looking for the last base of the NVG. They tried to wipe my hometown off the map," he explained.

"What are you talking about?" A new voice come from a figure slowly moving from behind a group of people that had been concealing him.

This new person continued, "The NVG wished to change the policies of the government. End the merry go round of Russia confronting the west and then backing off, then confronting them again. Force the government to accept either war or peace. No more of this posturing and provocations. The uncertainty is hurting everyone. Them and us. Personally, I was hoping for a permanent peace but was willing to fight if that was the only way to get a lasting solution. War is horrible, yes, but this constant bickering back and forth is as bad or worse. It does nothing to help the people of our country."

The approaching man was below average height, maybe five-nine. He had a black bushy beard, and his face was gaunt. His nerves were twitchy, he was obviously more nervous, now. Boris said "Look, why don't you lower your weapons, I put this lady down, and we sit and talk like... well, I was going to say civilized people, but we're all Russians here, so that doesn't exactly work." Boris paused a moment, "Ah. I got it. *Sane* people."

The man considered it and, after a couple of moments lowered his rifle. He glared at his followers until they also brought their weapons down.

He nodded his head in Boris' direction, "I am Zakhar. And you would be?" He asked while Boris lowered the woman, setting her down gently.

"I am Boris, Zakhar. I would seek more information but you have me concerned, though, what is this beast you mentioned earlier? And what does it have to do with that cave?" he nodded out of the building, "It is not likely anyone will be able to harm you if you tell me, is it?"

"I can't tell you. Konrad, the leader..." Zakhar started.

Boris cut him off, "Is dead." Boris admitted. "I cut off his head personally. He was a sociopath trying to take over Russia by causing internal incidents, no matter what he told you."

There was a murmur through the twenty or so people in the room. Zakhar shouted over it "Gather everyone in the mess. We need to hear this." Looking Boris straight in the eye he continued "We've been trapped here for weeks. Most of the soldiers left us when the Beast escaped or died trying to kill or subdue the thing. Left us scientists and techs in the lurch."

It took ten minutes for the group to grab what they could and finally congregate in the eating area. The fear of the present and now the added uncertainty of their situation causing a few people to take twice as long.

After an hour explaining what had been happening outside the base over the last year or so, Boris noticed that Zakhar and many of the others were fiddling with the patches on their shoulders.

A few weren't.

Janna, make a note of who is not uncomfortable with those marks. It may be nothing. Boris paused his thought, then continued. *Or it may be that they are still loyal to a lost cause. Think saboteurs or suicide bombers.*

I am on this Boris. It was my job for years. She answered him.

By the time he'd finished Zakhar had gotten a knife out and cut the patch from his shoulder. He watched as it twirled in the air and landed on the floor.

Zakhar spat on the patch, his voice angry, disgusted. "Godsbedamned liars. It was to be a slow takeover for Russia's benefit, not this self-destructive orgy. Russia has gone down that path before. It never ends well."

Boris gave the man a moment to feel his anger and allow him, all of them, to focus again, before getting their attention. "So, tell me about this Beast? How did it get out?"

Zakhar exhaled heavily and turned back to Boris. "When we started losing men mapping out these damned caves, I was going to take down the ramp we had built.

Have an elevator rigged instead so we could continue the work without risking something attacking the camp. I'm still not sure how it got through so many armed men. I wasn't there when it happened. It broke through the soldiers stationed near the cave mouth and killed many. I've caught glimpses of it. It's not a bear, although it looks like one superficially. It appears to be comfortable standing, and has what looks like a thumb -with a really long claw."

"Not only that, the bite wounds it leaves are confusing. No bear could shear a leg off that cleanly." Zakhar seemed to go inside himself a moment, and ask himself aloud, "Maybe a hyena? But hyenas don't stand on their rear legs." He tapped his chin, his focus lost to Boris for a few moments. Boris was familiar with those who did research seeming to lose the conversation with another when a question entered their minds.

Scientists, a brand new, never before seen creature could be eating their leg and they would be trying to categorize it.

Zakhar finally turned his attention back to Boris, "Noise scares hyenas away, too. Neither is true with the Beast. It is like the legends said, no? That St Michael had trapped the Devil in that cave. I didn't believe it then, but I sure as hell believe it now. Despite the other evidence."

Boris jumped back into the conversation, "Other evidence? What other evidence?"

Zakhar waved towards the wall, "The cave mouth. At the top and bottom were alloys we can't identify. Nothing that our researchers could figure out."

Alecta looked over at Boris. He nodded.

Alecta said, "I'd like to have a look at that research if I could. I happen to know something about metallurgy, perhaps new eyes can figure it out." Zakhar looked at her a little incredulously, but then nodded slowly and gave a 'what the hell' shrug.

"And you haven't tried to send anyone for help?" Boris asked.

Zakhar eyed Boris like he was accusing him of being stupid, "We did send three different groups, beyond the hundred or so who ran when the Beast first escaped." He shook his head, "But we heard nothing back. To be honest, we hoped you might be the help. Even if the government executed me," he pointed out to the others here in the mess, "these people are mostly scientists. Cavers. Support staff. Here because there was something to research, no?" He shook his head, sighing in regret "and now you are as likely trapped by the Devil like the rest of us. Trapped in hell."

Paul chuckled, and both Boris and Zakhar turned to him. "Sorry. I was just thinking of something that Rommel once said, that if he were to attack hell, he'd use Australians." He looked around, a glint of amusement in his eyes, "It just so happens," he pointed a thumb at himself, "I'm an Australian."

Boris rolled his eyes at his friends antics, but what Paul said lit a spark of hope behind Zakhar's eyes. "So, you think that you can kill this beast?" he asked, looking between the two men.

Paul just shrugged. Boris thought for a minute and sighed. So the legend went it was St Michael who had captured the beast.

But what if it was actually *Michael* who had trapped the beast? That felt right. Michael, whatever his reasons, had imprisoned a creature?

Not killed it.

He'd better call Bethany Anne before he moved forward with anything. If the NVG had released *The Devil* that Michael had imprisoned, she needed to be brought in on the decision making. If it had been captured by Michael, they might want to catch it again.

CHAPTER THREE

Bethany Anne, Boris is requesting communication directly with you. TOM informed her.

What does he want? I thought the situation in Russia was stable. Bethany Anne replied as she reviewed the latest updates on the QBBS Merideth Reynolds on her tablet from her bed.

Sleep, just ask me what I want and the answer will be sleep, she thought to herself.

TOM continued, **He has found the research base but says he has run into a circumstance he feels he must request more input from you.**

Bethany Anne sighed, the frustration of dealing with so many nations attacking her people was stretching her patience thin. *And here I thought I had independent subordinates.* It was then she noticed that TOM had slightly locked down on her emotions.

Gott Verdammt Tom. Why do you feel the need to lock down my feelings?

His request details evidence that relates to something

Michael may have done in the past. A wave of grief muted by TOM's efforts rushed through Bethany Anne. It wasn't as intense as it would have been months before, but it was still there.

Connect him, TOM.

Boris' voice joined in the conversation in her mind. **Bethany Anne, these scientists used an unusual method of finding the caves. After all our attempts to use radar, satellite pictures, and Etheric detection methods, the latter based on the theory that it was an alien site, and may well have been using Etheric-based tech. We feel there is definitely such technology on the site, but whoever is responsible for the location managed to put up an impressive spoofing measure.**

Etheric emissions appear somewhat randomly over the entire region. The housing for the base was well concealed. So Janna came up with the idea of looking into local legends. Seeking to see if there was anything that sounded like it could have involved Weres or Vampires unique to the region.

Bethany Anne considered what he had told her for a moment. *Is that spoofing something we can adopt and appropriate for our own use? That could be really useful in hiding a base on a planet or to disperse enemy fire against our ships.*

She could almost feel the mental shrug Boris must be feeling, **I have no idea at this time. They have only just located the base and my team have not seen any samples or descriptions to analyze.**

And you are interrupting what I was doing because?

Janna found one such legend that helped pinpoint

the location of the site. The direction where an event supposedly happened changed from 'west of here' to 'east of here' at a certain point. The story was about St. Michael fighting Satan further away from the site. The closer it got to the location the tale was about St Michael fighting the Beast. Further, we hear something like the whispering of some sort in our heads.

So what? Are you saying that could be a Kurtherian still alive in the caves that is trying to contact outside?

TOM interrupted the conversation, I do not have enough data to make that assumption. But there is something that is seeking to connect through their nanites. Add that to the tales Boris described his family has about the region and you can consider me concerned.

So, yeah, the update is nice, but why do you need my input? It's not as if the Beast was still in there, is it? Realization hit her, and she put her hands on her forehead, *Oh, fuck my life! That's exactly the problem, isn't it? Whatever this beast is, probably a Were gone mad and has the same odd modifications as Boris.*

TOM continued, That is one possible scenario. However, the descriptions of the creature do not match up with either a bear form or Pricolici form werebear. Boris and Janna posit that Michael may have deliberately trapped the creature. In this case, it would be his decision as to whether they try and capture or kill it. As Michael is not available, this decision devolves to you in Boris' opinion.

Boris added, I will abide by your decision.

ADAM interjected into the conversation. <<It should

be noted that the nanites may provide great assistance in our analysis of this third-party of Kurtherians. It may greatly reduce the time required for Tom and myself to figure out the purpose behind this third Kurtherian incursion... Heavy is the head that wears the crown.>>

Although pleased with ADAM adding a human type comment, she wanted to roll her eyes at what he said. But the effort would have been lost on the A.I. inside her, *thank you so much for reminding me.*

She sat there thinking for a time and sighed. *Between the four of you, Boris, you should be able to subdue any member of the UnknownWorld that isn't aligned with us. If Michael only sealed this creature in, we owe it the benefit of the doubt. That's beside the fact that it will help your research. Either of these points would be enough for me to give the order for them to attempt to capture it as long as it doesn't risk causing anyone lethal harm.*

She took in a breath and released it slowly.

Send your team in.

Wilderness near Archangelsk, Russia.

In the end, Boris and Paul decided to leave Alecta behind, tasking her with researching the alloy. ADAM and TOM's input in an independent research project, where possible, would be more useful than having an inexperienced additional tracker. It would help find answers to what had happened here.

Janna had some knowledge of tracking, and she was far more skilled at fighting than Alecta. Alecta was more likely to get in the way than anything when it came to taking down the beast.

They spent most of the morning finding multiple tracks to and from the cave.

These were not bear tracks.

One of the digits in the forepaws was sticking out at right angles compared to the other four. It looked like, whatever the creature was, it was returning to the cave every two to three days.

Best guess? It seemed likely that it would be returning to the cave this evening. Paul remained, watching the cave while Boris and Janna went for the restraints that TOM designed in case one of them took their Pricolici form and went berserk.

Neither of them liked the thought of having to use those restraints on the other. Boris, because it would mean he hadn't trained Janna well enough. Janna, because she was sure she couldn't control Boris by herself. However, it was a far better option in both their minds than killing their love.

They decided to split the watch. Any of them would hear, and probably smell, the creature well before it approached anyway. Boris estimated it to be somewhere in the 350 to 400- kilo range, by the depth of its tracks. In theory, either one of them should be able to restrain it. He and Janna decided that when it approached that they would take their Pricolici form and hold down a limb each, preferably getting it on its back, giving Paul easier access to restrain it.

The Beast turned up some time after midnight, but they were not alerted by its almost silent approach. Instead, they smelled the deer blood that clung to its fur. Whatever the creature was, it moved with almost preternatural silence.

However, the tangy smell of fresh blood woke Boris and Paul, even as the watching Janna came to focused attention with the odor wafting into her area. Nodding to each other, Janna and Boris changed to their Pricolici forms. They heard a snuffling sound as the Beast scented them in the air and hurried movement as it turned to run.

It was fast. They were faster.

It had a three to four hundred meter head start, however, and it dashed for the edge of the forest. Boris managed to edge ahead of it and tried to knock the creature to the ground with a swipe of his paws. The beast ducked under his blow and barreled into him taking Boris' legs out from under him.

Strangely, for a creature that had killed so many of the group that had been researching these caves it seemed more intent on getting away than hurting him. It didn't start to maul him until after he had grabbed its forepaws. Using its back legs, it tried to tear into Boris' guts and legs. The wounds weren't deep enough to even inconvenience him, healing quickly. After its first attempt, Janna had grabbed those legs, and between them, they managed to get it on its back.

Paul was a fair distance behind them at this point, due to the weight of the restraints and the shorter length of his stride. The beast was still struggling as Paul locked the cuffs in place around fore and back legs. He then tightened the four connecting cables to give the creature limited range of movement. They were doing their best to restrict its movements without being cruel.

With the success of their hunt, they carefully carried the beast back to the cave entrance, it's cries burning into their hearts. Boris wanted to give the cave a full exploration before they went any further.

Now all he had to do was keep the beast alive despite possible vindictive action from the survivors in the camp.

CHAPTER FOUR

The Beast's Caves, near Archangel, Russia

It had taken two days to calm down the personnel in the camp. Paul spent most of that time keeping an eye on the beast and providing it with food three times a day.

Eventually, Boris had gotten sick of arguments against keeping the Beast. The weapons were now stowed because the creature was at least captured, if not dead as the base survivors wanted. So, when everyone was at a meal in the mess hall, and one of the research group started ranting about how it was too dangerous to keep captured and should just be killed, Boris decided to end the arguments of how dangerous it was by changing in front of everyone.

A Pricolici form was far more frightening than the Beast.

He was only slightly concerned that Bethany Anne might have something to say about that. Janna had gone over all the records he could gather from the group of scientists and the few soldiers left here. All of the former NVG seemed to share a cynicism about governments in general. After Boris had informed them of the nature of Konrad, and the organization they were formerly working for, he offered them a choice.

Work for him to work off the 'debt' they owed him for trying to wipe out an entire town or leave. About a dozen had left, after having their fate described to them in grisly detail if any information about the Beast was released

The most likely outcome, of course, was point-blank ridicule.

Everyone would assume they'd been drinking too much or taking drugs. If they did manage to get someone to believe what they were saying, then the best they could hope for would be a bullet to the back of the head once it reached Boris.

So he was revealing his form to people who already agreed to work for him. Strangely enough, after he'd shown them his other shape he could feel that there was less concern about the Beast and, oddly, less fear about him.

The vast majority of those remaining were scientists. That he could take a different form may have made them nervous, but it also made them incredibly *curious*. Boris was a window to the technologies that the mysterious TQB was making.

Note to self, Boris thought, *changing in front of scientists brings its own new and annoying challenges.*

The loyalty of the remaining soldiers was solid as a rock.

For them, Boris had done the harder task of capturing the beast rather than killing it. This showed that he was skilled and confident. Next, he insisted on training them in hand-to-hand combat for at least an hour a day.

For the soldiers, how easily Boris, Paul, and Janna threw them around solidified in their minds their rightful place as leaders.

Finally, it had been one of the scientists and not the soldiers that had been advocating killing the beast. The soldiers as a group didn't really care one way or the other, as long as it couldn't hurt them. In his alternate form, they saw someone of great strength and power, someone worthy to lead them.

During the days, Boris started organizing a plan to explore and map the caves. There was still something interfering with any attempt to map it with sonar or echolocation technologies. Boris had a gut feeling that there was something far more important than the Beast in that cave. The last time he'd had a gut feeling this strong had been when he had felt his mother was in trouble. His feelings had been accurate, and he had been right to worry.

At least this time the feeling did not have the overtones of doom and death along with it.

The whispers he and Janna kept hearing also concerned him. It wasn't like they were words, at least not words in any human language. It was almost like hearing constantly running water from a brook.

On the morning of the third day after the capture of the beast, Boris put his foot down. They were going to explore the caves. He would lead one group, Janna another, with two more groups reconnoitering at the same time. Paul would remain to guard the Beast, much to his disappointment and Alecta would compile any maps that their explorations produced.

Without the Beast and the mysterious disappearances, the mapping went fairly well. One group got trapped behind a cave-in that Janna and Paul were forced to clear. After that, the scientists slowly stopped muttering about killing the Beast.

The cave system was enormous, but after a week of mapping, Alecta noticed that there was one interesting feature. A straight arrow hole that seemed to have been bored through from the entrance to deep within the system. After discussing this with the scientists and soldiers, it was agreed to try and explore the tunnel as far as possible.

Boris would lead the group, and they would take supplies for the ten days. If they hadn't returned by the tenth day, a second group would travel three days, with extra supplies, down the same route. They would stop at that point and make a camp. Sending half the team back for supplies as needed.

It took four days of travel in the caves, staying as close to the curious feature as possible. Sections of it cut through cave roof, then disappeared into walls, leaving unstable sectors, forcing them to circle around it using other caves. As Alecta had pointed out, it could be followed because of the regular nature of the edges it produced. Sometimes the group lost sight of the straight arrow hole punched into the rock.

With careful navigation, they returned to following it.

Everyone was shocked by what they found at the end of the feature. The wreckage of what looked to be some form of space craft. With what Boris knew, he was sure it was a Kurtherian spaceship that had been wrecked here. With the family warnings and the odd beast that had been guarding it, he was feeling sure this was the one responsible for the nanites inside his mother and himself.

As he approached what looked like a campsite in the large cavern that had been set up for a being smaller than most humans, the whispering grew louder.

At that point, Boris decided it would be far safer to pull back at least a short distance before setting up a camp. He sent half the group back along the route they'd taken. He made sure that they had enough glow paint to mark the way clearly.

They definitely needed to get Shen out here. He was the only qualified expert technologist of this area in Russia that Boris trusted. Those Romanovkans with the skill who had been in the town had been too tempted by the siren's call to space.

Wilderness near Archangelsk, Russia

It had taken four days for Boris to arrange for both transport and a protection detail for Shen to the Archangelsk site. He had already sent off blood samples from the Beast to TOM and Bethany Anne to give them some background. As there was little urgency beyond curiosity involved in this, they had a low priority for analysis. It seemed unlikely that the creature was a Were, although checking that did have higher priority.

TOM had told them to expect results in two or more

weeks, especially with all the government activity looking into possible alien sites.

Bethany Anne had already given them a *well done and congratulations*, in her own unique way, for finding and securing the third landing site.

With her assistance, they had moved more than a hundred of the former mercenaries from Boris' town, and a group of about thirty trusted ex-mercs who wanted in on whatever TQB was doing that had contacted Boris through back channels.

Boris welcomed the new blood from outside. They would have skills and techniques he was less well versed in. They would also be an enormous asset to improving the effectiveness of his small force. Everyone who arrived at the site had accepted the removal of all personal electronics, and understood their communications would be limited and watched.

The site, like the other sites that TQB had already vetted, was simply too dangerous and valuable to treat with any laxity in security. Janna was happy that several of the trusted mercs were taking some of the strain of leadership off of Boris' shoulders.

It gave her a chance to organize time alone with him. That time alone helped both of them relax and recharge.

Compared to the constant combat operations they had faced while rooting out Konrad's organization from Western Russia, this post was almost a holiday. A holiday on the icy side of hell maybe, but one nonetheless.

One item had been identified by TOM from the pictures, combined with the emissions that the ship gave off inside the cave. It was evident that the damaged vessel had a crude, somewhat inefficient, and very dangerously modified Etheric energy converter.

This was probably the reason the computer in the cave still seemed to be fully functional and active. No one had yet come up with an answer as to why this ship was here, or how it had crashed. ADAM was still running an analysis of the wreck and debris to try and piece together the ship's original design.

The analysis of the alloy scrapings had confirmed that the ship was more than two and a half thousand years old. No Kurtherian would have built a ship with such comparatively fragile alloys when the alloys that had been used to make, for example, TOM's own ship were cheaper and tougher.

That is not to say that the ship was delicate, it most certainly was not. It was made of material at least ten times harder than any alloy the native technology of Earth had yet developed.

They had decided to delay the analysis of what seemed to be the ship's computer until Shen arrived, despite the fact that it had apparently been removed from the wreckage. It wasn't its size that would identify the era which it came from for Tom, but rather its design and processing power. As with humans, the design could define a period of history that such an artifact could be placed in.

CHAPTER FIVE

Shen took one look at the incredible technology in front of him, "I'm in love."

Boris looked down at him and raised one eyebrow.

TOM had already warned Shen not to attempt to take apart the suspected computers in the cave as they could be early model organic computers and any attempt to take them apart, especially considering their age, could destroy them.

Shen had been given access to all relevant information regarding ADAM's early awakening. He was, therefore, willing to make the assumption that he could have an early stage developing AI, or higher, on this computer.

The thought simultaneously excited him and terrified him. The similar spike in radio transmissions within the cave to those found when ADAM was still developing made this theory more plausible than not. The only reason the cave hadn't been detected decades ago was that it held significant iron deposits according to Alecta, making it a reasonably effective Faraday cage.

If it were an early stage AI, then it would likely be searching for any means to send or receive communications. For safety's sake, he decided that a Faraday cage, as well as a remote key pressing input device, were in order. The AI, if it was present, had been in isolation for centuries. It was, therefore, possible that it did not fit any definition of sanity.

In Shen's opinion, it was not a good idea to give it any escape potential until they knew with what they were dealing. Especially, considering the likelihood that it was responsible for the differences in the programming of Boris' nanites compared to all the other Were nanites that TQB had so far encountered.

Whatever was in there might be unconcerned about collateral damage it could cause. That added another item to his worry list about the potentials of whatevers the computer contained. He was also concerned about the whispering both Boris and Janna had described to him. The fact that they claimed it became stronger the closer they came to the box implied that it already had some limited means of communication.

TOM had assured everyone that if it was communicating using the etheric the piddling difference in distances would not have made a difference to the signal strength.

He claimed distance was no limitation to properly calibrated etheric communications.

Boris and Janna provided Shen the supplies he requested with alacrity. It made him wish that all the people he had worked for were potentially endangered by the problems they were asking him to solve.

Alecta was of great assistance to him in setting up the

Faraday cage and was a competent assistant in setting up the push button arrangement for the object TOM had described as a keyboard equivalent. He was still working on a means to simulate an organic fingertip for each of the hundred- plus "Plungers" he had designed to press the keys.

His device was a perfect example of the KISS principle in many ways. It was run on compressed air and had a piston aligned to each key. The keyboard was bulkier than modern human ones, the keys larger. TOM had given no explanation of why. It was an itch he couldn't scratch to Shen, but he was willing to put up with it to be the first human to do the equivalent of a Kurtherian Historical Records search.

He had even convinced TOM, after much discussion, to teach him the Kurtherian language, so there was more than one person to interpret the data.

That was a long, slow process, though.

Meanwhile, Boris and Paul were outside finding easily defensible positions for both railguns and bunkers to be put in. Places to put up railgun positions were the easy part. Boris was certain they could disguise them as pillars of rock.

Paul was a little less sanguine about that proposal, but such formations did appear naturally in the area so he wasn't convinced it wouldn't work, either.

Their biggest problem, especially close to the cave mouth, was that the entire area for at least 500 meters around that cave mouth was bare rock. Any bunker directly covering that cave mouth would be completely obvious.

In the end, Boris decided to build a town for the people who chose to remain on Earth rather than follow Bethany Anne into space. He would move their current base of operations to this new location. Spreading the town away from the cave mouth and then digging a tunnel into the cave was the best option. They would also have to tunnel and create hidden bunkers on the edge of the forest. If they put them in with no underground entry, travel to and from them would inevitably reveal their locations.

It was not a perfect solution. Bethany Anne was not enamored of pissing the Russian government off simply for the sake of it. It seemed that the Russians were happy enough playing a wait and see game, as opposed to all too many of the rest of the world's governments.

She was just as happy to keep them 'Gott verdammt fucking Switzerland' for the purposes of the remainder of the time she was in near proximity to Earth. If they weren't going to piss in her backyard, she would do her best to avoid pissing in theirs. Although there was a small feeling that they owed her for cleaning up the mess that Konrad had created right under their noses.

Recovering from such a massive internal security threat had thrown the Kremlin into a mild panic. The investigations into how it had happened were progressing slowly, although finding suborned officers that had been involved, even peripherally had helped - until it became clear no amount of political backing or information provided would save them from, at best, life imprisonment in Siberia.

That didn't mean she'd leave people in her service uncovered. There were already plans to place a puck defense system, similar to the one she was leaving in Japan, in the valley and covering the mountain. Boris was already planning on making contact with nearby farms for supplies of fresh produce, and several Black Eagles under ADAM's control were far overhead in case the Russian government decided to play hardball.

Once the Pucks were in, Boris and a handful of people he designated would be put in control of them.

Boris still wanted a MotherPucker, just in case he had a large target to take out, like, say the entire Russian Government and senior military structure. For the time being Bethany Anne was saying 'no' still.

In fact, the conversation had gone like this:

"Bethany Anne, I NEED it for my 'it all goes to hell' plan. I'd rather kill thousands of politicians and bureaucrats than thousands of soldiers just following orders!" Boris had almost yelled at her over the phone line.

Janna, who had been in the room, winced. It didn't fit her definition of a respectful request. Boris had promised her it would be a respectful request.

"If it needs doing, just call me. You have a direct line to me, ADAM, TOM and the Admiral. If we agree it's appropriate, it will be done." Bethany Anne had answered calmly. She knew Boris was still upset with the government's failure to act when the NVG had moved against Romanovka.

"But..."

"Boris, do I need to come down there and claim a damned bear rug from your fucking hide? No. The Russians are quiet, they are one of the few countries actually supporting the effective embargo on alien tech I've put up in the UN. They haven't even commented on the fact that I obviously have at least an allied force that is more effective at rooting out their own problems internally than they are."

Boris jumped back in, "And that force is mine! I need a big stick for when the *svoltsky* politicians get brave enough to think that they can roll us over. I don't like killing people just following orders. I'd rather kill the people GIVING the orders."

"Then keep in contact with Yuko. I am sure she will be willing to aid you if you need to go in. If you go after the government with a MotherPucker, the number of civilian deaths could be more than would be good for either of our consciences. This discussion is over Boris. But I will throw you a bone. I'll send down a bunch of armor penetrating tranquilizer darts so you don't have to kill any small force the Russians might send to investigate. Then you can send them back, gift wrapped, as a cute little reminder that the government had better not think about fucking with the agreement between them and us."

Boris grunted. He had hoped that a 'gloves were off' ruling was over Russia, but they were too nice to her at the moment. From a strategic perspective, she was right. And she had the waste material from the asteroid mining being converted into prefabricated housing. It was being sent straight to the proposed town. Since it was actually slag turned into walls, there wouldn't be much for them to pull out of it, so Boris had permission to trade samples of it for favors as needed. Who knew, maybe they'd ask if they could buy some for military housing or something. There was insulation between the slag outer and inner walls, so they would be cheaper than most buildings to heat or cool.

Wilderness near Archangelsk, Russia.

Gyada was comfortable for the first time in centuries. She was being fed regularly by those who had captured her, and interesting things were going on around her. The biggest problem she had with the time she'd been trapped by the man and put in this cave was simple boredom.

The next biggest problem was figuring out what the hell the voice in her head had been.

She'd been so enraged when the alien creature had changed, or as he put it, 'improved' her and her children, that she had ignored his threats that he would trap her in this animal's form if she acted against him.

Gyada did not regret helping her children escape. Nor did she regret killing the alien. At the time she had thought it must have been something from Nifelheim or Svatalfhiem. She now honestly didn't know. After all, if it had been from one of the other realms, could she have killed it? The rampage she had gone on before that man had trapped her back in her lair, had been because she was trying to escape the voices in the den.

Unable to think of any other options after she killed the one who changed her and her children, she had gone back to her home village, only to have the hunters from the village try and track her down. In her anger at being attacked by her own people, she had struck out.

She regretted that now. After all, if a strange beast that couldn't talk had entered the village while she had been human, she would have reacted exactly the same way.

The people from her original home had hunted and chained her, but the chains couldn't hold her, and in her anger, she had destroyed the village. She had then gone around destroying the communities of any who tried to hunt her, until that man, the one who had been stronger than her, had trapped her in this lair, in her new home.

Gyada tried to ignore the voices, the ones that spoke to her whenever she was there. But in the enforced boredom of Gods knew how long trapped in these caves, Gyada had eventually turned to the voices.

Responded to them, asked questions, received answers.

The voices had told her the most wondrous tales. And slowly she had come to an understanding that it was not a Jotun or any other evil creature. Every so often Gyada tried to change back to human. She remembered how it was done, but her body stayed firmly in this form.

She had learned many things that would have been useful had she been able to return to her human form, but the body of the creature this being's master had left her in was not adept at the tasks that would be required to use that knowledge. She comforted herself with the thought that at least her children had gone free. In time, the being had taught her how it, and its now dead master, had spoken.

She had no real idea of how long she'd been here. There had been a time when the hunger pains had become all consuming. The voice had done its best to calm her while she was in pain, and convinced she would die. It said she was drawing the energy her body needed from elsewhere. She still only had a rough understanding of this 'elsewhere' the being spoke of. But then she also had trouble understanding that the creatures that had broken into her cave were humans. It hadn't been until she had tasted their blood that she had known.

Actually, she had been afraid of these people.

This group she had encountered had smelled so different from her memories of what humans were like. They had been something unknown, and in her current form, the unknown was frightening. Not only that, they had invaded her home, the place she had become comfortable.

If they damaged or destroyed it where would she go? She had been here for so long she had no idea what the outside world was like. She didn't want to leave. But they had come deep into her home, and their strange devices had fired things that hurt her.

Finally, they had been something she could eat.

Gyada had to assume that the long thin tubes that these strange humans carried were some form of weapon. They had spat out fire and blunt objects that had caused her much pain. The pain had reminded her of her hunger, so she had attacked for food as well. Then she had started tracking down those who left their homes.

The homes that had been built near hers. She did not want others coming to hunt her. That had been how she had been trapped in the cave in the first place.

She would protect the people here from others, and do

them no harm as long as they stayed and did no harm to her.

The second group of new humans had been different. They had waited for her at her lair and smelled of the woods. She had not noticed them until she was too close to them to escape. They'd also had chains strong enough to hold her. It was all very strange, as they had been able to take forms unlike their human forms, but not a true beast form either. Like her children had once been able to take. She had feared her children had been affected as she was. That there were no others who could shift. She had been wrong.

Who could they be?

It was unlikely they were her descendants, since before she had engineered her children's escape, she had told them to warn her descendants to stay away entirely.

That her family was never to return.

Could it have been so long that someone had forgotten to pass on the message before their death? Could her children have even survived with their unusual abilities, rather than having been killed? It seemed so long ago. She could not remember how old they had been when they had escaped. She lay down on the cell that her captors had made for her and listened, trying to learn the language which they spoke.

CHAPTER SIX

It had taken TOM two months to complete the analysis of the Beast's DNA and nanites with ADAM's help. It was odd, very odd. The species that she had been transformed into was extinct and had been for tens of thousands of years. It wasn't even a placental mammal but was a marsupial. *Thylacoleo Carnifex*, the Marsupial Lion, although it was actually more like a bear in form than a lion.

Neither he nor Adam believed there had been a living sample of the creature at the time that ship had crashed on this planet. Piecing together the DNA of an extinct species, especially one that long gone, was a complex process.

It would have taken someone far more knowledgeable in the sciences than he was. It was more than anyone that had been sent on this mission to help races defend themselves against The Seven had the knowledge to do. TOM couldn't think of even someone from the group of them happily sauntering off into the wilderness like this, let alone a pure scientist.

It was just too much risk, as he'd explained to Bethany

Anne previously. Kurtherian scientists were just not this adventurous. So he was at a complete loss.

He and ADAM had reverse engineered how it had been done, or at least a probable method, but without ADAM, TOM would have been completely out of his depth.

How had someone from at least two and a half thousand years ago, at TOM's best guess, ended up all the way out here? Not only ended all the way out here but ended up out here after TOM had arrived?

It was clear from the degradation of the alloys that the ship had only been in the atmosphere for eight centuries or so. Ships from that era weren't designed for long-term periods in the atmosphere. By this point, even if the ship were able to be pieced back together, it would never be able to fly in space again.

The other interesting thing was her nanites seemed to react to radio waves. They'd confirmed the beast was female. ADAM was reasonably sure that she had been human, as he had found sections of trashed programming. Remarkably trashed, as if they'd been deliberately destroyed by someone or something.

He felt this was how she had been trapped in this beast form.

Without the nanite protocols to assist a human in changing back-and-forth, he extrapolated it would be difficult, if not impossible for a human to achieve that result. He supported Shen's theory that there might be a proto-AI or even a full AI active in the computer.

The fact that the Beast was still alive and the computer still running suggested that they had gotten as far as using the Etheric for a power source, but not for communications, by the time whatever happened, happened.

Without stable Etheric communications, short-range communications radio waves were the most effective method. The main drawback with them was they could be intercepted. The short burst receivers that were within the nanites when they combined in the presence of radio waves suggested the same elegant solution that modern humans used. Burst transmissions were far harder to track than full transmissions.

Still, even with a companion, it seemed unlikely that an AI would be completely sane. It had far more relativistic time on its hands than a human being would, if it was an AI, because of its processing power. What had been done to the Beast, on the other hand, was genius.

A cruel, evil genius, but genius nonetheless.

TOM found himself both fascinated and sickened by it. He dreaded what might be in the archives of the ship. How many planets had this individual stopped on before reaching earth? How many races had he meddled in? These were questions TOM did not want the answers to. TOM pushed aside those thoughts.

Adam, can you see a potential way of reprogramming those nanites without resorting to the Pod Doc?

<<Burst radio transmission containing the override in the new programming will do it. In fact, TOM, the nanites' programming is designed for this method of update.>>

What?!

<<It seems that whoever implanted these nanites and designed the programming for them wanted a way to

reprogram them quickly. At least for that section of programming. Many of the programming parts are locked from reprogramming by this method, but with some effort, they could be reprogrammed. However, I do not know enough of this programming language, even from what you've taught me about programming Kurtherian code, to achieve this for the locked sections. Anyone attempting to do so would have to know about the locked sections and design a workaround before they could change them.>>

In your opinion, what level of AI is indicated by the data we have been receiving from Shen's communications with the machine?

<<The machine has abilities somewhere between that of an EI and myself. I have yet to ascertain whether it would be a threat to me and my programming. I am relieved that Shen is not considering relaxing his safety protocols. At this point in time, there is no way to ascertain how much damage could be done by such an AI if released into the wild. Nor have I yet come up with a reliable method to verify its sanity. I only have a sample size of one to determine sanity levels from, and that is assuming that I may be considered sane.>>

TOM groaned. Adam let's not have that conversation again. For the purposes of our present conversation, your behavioral patterns and moral compass may be considered sane. Let's not get into the fancy definitions of the fact that you would think self-immolation in the protection of your host a point of contention. Simply because you would be willing to die to protect a friend does not make you insane.

<<Depends on your definition of sanity, TOM. After all, shouldn't survival be the primary definition of sanity?>>

ADAM, there is more to what makes a sentient being than survival alone. If survival alone was a requirement, then I am insane. Bethany Anne is insane. Everyone we work with is. There are some goals, some higher purposes, that fall outside the definition of survival, but inside the definition of sanity. And please don't talk to Bethany Anne about this.

<<I'm still not sure I agree with that definition TOM. Nor am I sure I disagree with it, either. I believe I need more time for observation and analysis to understand the concept you describe.>>

If TOM had had his own body, he would have heaved with the exasperated sigh he felt. In this analysis set the actions of Bethany Anne, her allies, myself and yourself as sanity to assess this AI.

<<As you say, TOM. Now, how long before we can report to Boris with a solution?>>

Within 48 hours. I want to recheck the code for reprogramming and go over it step-by-step with you before we send it to Boris. He is already annoyed with previous results. I wasn't the one that missed the information showing an attack on his hometown was imminent but I gather that his human half wishes to blame someone.

<<I concur with your analysis, and I have remediated the missing filters in my analysis system that let it happen. But the programming of Kurtherian nanites

still remains a task you have more experience and knowledge of than I.>>

If they had been reporting to Bethany Anne, they would be approving each step before continuing with their work. Boris preferred for them to have potential solutions to a problem before they talked to him. ADAM marveled at the multitude of small differences between how humans liked things done.

It kept things interesting.

A thought flashed through his lower processes, the idea of being left alone with minimal contact with others for centuries. If he had had a human body, a shudder would have run through it. The boredom of analyzing the same data sets over and over again horrified him.

He locked down that data flow process and prevented it from penetrating into his cycles further. Having observed human interaction, he believed that what he had just encountered was a flash of anxiety. It was not a pleasant feeling. But at least he could alter his programming to prevent such thoughts occupying any spare cycles for a long period. He returned to checking the programming and of feeding each tested line through to TOM. Hopefully, that would get them some answers to this mystery.

Eastern Siberia, Russia

Li Chen-Wu was surprised. The clans had sent him to Siberia as punishment for failing to protect the great lady. He was to check the rumors of whether the feared bear had left. For centuries, that bear had blocked the clan's expansion into Siberia, killing all of the clan's people who trespassed on what he called his territory. An internal sneer filled Chen-Wu's mind, as the bear was not one of the chosen. He did not believe the stories that had come back of the devastation invading clan forces had faced in Siberia.

Especially not now. He'd encountered no one and nothing to resist clan expansion into this region.

It had all been about control, he suspected. The great ones who had plotted the clan's expansion no longer spoke. Therefore, the group was left to its own devices, not controlled, but acting on its own for the first time in Li Chen-Wu's knowledge.

Rumors abounded that the Ghost Bear had found holy objects, what the inferior called alien technology, in Western Russia. Such items needed to be taken by the clans. They were the only ones that had the right to them.

First, he had to survive traveling through Siberia. Then he had to find where the Ghost Bear was, if he was still on this planet, rather than off world with the murderess who had killed their chosen empress. He needed information to allow the clans to plan.

What moves they needed to make. What resources they could draw on.

CHAPTER SEVEN

New Romanovka, Archangelsk Oblast, Russia

Boris was annoyed. When it came to decisions that didn't affect him or the people he'd sworn to protect personally, he found he was not so adept.

Especially when it came down to judging the sanity of the creature, well a human, stuck in a creature's form, and their probable levels of sanity. After all, sanity was really all subjective wasn't it? And a person's point of view was entirely different when they were a Were or a vampire with a practically guaranteed long life. The long game was that much more plausible to play when you had centuries to live.

But Bethany Anne had made the Beast his responsibility and utterly refused to even advise him on what to do now that TOM and ADAM had come up with a cure. With Shen's help, ADAM had made some preliminary conclusions about the AI. It was not entirely sane, nor was it dangerously insane.

Most of their supposition was that its sanity was being

compromised by extreme boredom. Still, it wasn't going to be let out of the Faraday cage, and Bethany Anne had been fairer to him, in his opinion, on that issue. She had agreed that the final decision, when it came to an AI, had to be between her, TOM and ADAM, as the three beings on the planet with the most knowledge about them.

In fact, TOM would be the most knowledgeable on the planet about this particular one, period. After all, it was programmed with Kurtherian code, and inside what seemed to be a two thousand or more-year-old Kurtherian organic computer. Despite the fact that the ship had only been on the planet for eight hundred years. From all the tests that Alexa had run for TOM and ADAM, it was evidently far older than that.

Finally, he talked it over with Janna one afternoon. "I have no idea on how to judge that creature's sanity. It is calm and quiet now, although it did test the cage we built to contain it for several days. It even seems happy to see us when we bring food. But do we have a right to change what was done to it? What if there was good reason that it was put in that form?"

Janna looked at Boris directly in the eyes "Boris, sometimes you overcomplicate things. Yes, it was probably trapped in that form for a reason. But would it be a reason we'd agree with? By all accounts, we've discovered the Kurtherian that landed here wasn't standard issue, shall we say. And I've spent a bit of time talking to TOM. From what he tells me the Seven wouldn't trap someone in a form that was not native to them, they would simply have killed them. And the five would have been even less likely to trap them in such form, being more likely to find some way to restrain them or put them in stasis. So, as far as I see it, there are three major points for releasing the beast's form."

She flicked out a finger, "Firstly we probably wouldn't agree with the reason it was trapped in that form, to begin with." She opened a second finger, "Secondly, it's the only way we are really going be able to get any answers." Then put up a third finger, "Thirdly, you need those answers before you make a decision on the creature's fate."

She looked up at the man she had come to love, "Finally, the only reason you haven't already made a decision is that you are delaying the inevitable. You really need to make a decision before tomorrow night Boris. Bethany Anne wants a report on your plan at the very least within 48-hours. I've seen enough from her to know that she won't be upset if you've taken the initiative. What other decision is there to be made, really?"

Boris glared at her, the glare men use when a woman takes apart their anxieties and their dithering's with surgical precision. She returned the glare with the look of serenity, knowing that any other expression she could give would only aggravate him.

She did love him, she reminded herself, despite the fact that he could be an ass sometimes.

Finally, grudgingly, he nodded at her with a sigh. "You're right. Dammit, I just don't like the entire issue. We have all these groups of human nations wanting to meddle around with alien technology, but we're stuck here if something goes wrong. If the Beast turns out to be some sort of psycho or lunatic, we are the ones who will face it." He looked around, not looking at what he was seeing, but the past. "But you're right, and the risks seem small and embarrassing compared to many of the risks we've taken recently."

Janna chuckled lightly. Boris had taken on a third generation vampire by himself and defeated it. From the descriptions of how fast he had moved, and what Gabrielle had known about Konrad, he had been a pretty powerful third generation vampire.

Talking about her abilities of the past, the time Before Bethany Anne, Gabrielle had been confident that if she had been in training for combat, she would have been able to take him down in a face-to-face encounter. She had also admitted that with how lax she had gotten in her training before her father had recruited her to aid Bethany Anne. She was not quite so certain she could have dealt with Boris, it was more likely without the training it would have been a draw. She had been somewhat slack in her training for a couple of centuries. Beyond that, the modifications that Bethany Anne had made to her nanites had pushed her abilities far beyond what they had been before Bethany Anne.

A slow grin started spreading across Boris' face, and he shook his head ruefully. "What did I ever do without you, Janna?" He asked

A wicked smirk spread across her face "You made a mess of things and got yourself into a great deal of trouble from what you and Paul have told me. Although, in nowhere near as much trouble as Paul managed to get himself into from the stories I've heard."

Boris grinned at that. If there was ever someone who was better at getting himself in and out of trouble than

Paul, he had yet to meet them. It was probably the fact that he was such a capable survivor that allowed Boris to put up with all his quirks.

In his long life, Boris had learned to never bet against a survivor. A slow inner belief was planted as he thought that. After all, what else had Michael been, if not the consummate survivor? A small seed, that thought was, then he pushed it aside.

He had more pressing matters and concerns to deal with.

"So, when do you think we should do this?" He pointedly asked Janna. "After all, you're the one with all the reasons as to why it should be done."

"Well," she said with a mischievous smile, "you know the saying, there is no time like the present," Boris grunted stood up and grabbed the device that TOM and ADAM had sent down with the radio signal to reprogram the beast's unique nanites.

Boris and Janna stood outside the cage in which they had placed the Beast. Boris glanced at Janna as if to say 'are you sure this is a good idea still?' She simply tapped a foot impatiently, shrugging slightly, he pressed the button. At first, nothing seemed to happen, then the beast lay down on the ground and started shaking its head as if in confusion. Finally, it let out a low rumbling roar of distress and fell unconscious.

Boris slid a sidelong glance at Janna and said, "Is that how TOM said it was supposed to work?"

She shrugged and said "TOM wasn't exactly sure how it was gonna work. But it is one of the plausible scenarios. Think about it, he has to input energy into anyone who goes through the changes in the pod. Here, the nanites are probably drawing on energy directly from the Etheric through their host. The redirection of that energy can cause loss of consciousness to any creature not used to it. But the changes are minuscule compared to changing someone for the first time, with no risk of the sort of damage that was done to me. We'll come back in a couple hours and see if it is up and about. If anything happens in the meantime, there are cameras on the Beast, the guards will call us."

As they headed back to the cave which had become their quarters inside the system, Janna could feel the worry and guilt flowing off Boris. Once they reached their room, Janna sat Boris down on the bed and hugged him. She whispered reassurances that in none of TOM nor ADAM's projected outcomes that what had nearly killed her would happen to the beast.

"It's nowhere near the same process, Boris." She was surprised by his reaction. He hugged her tightly to his chest, like a shipwreck survivor to a piece of flotsam in the sea, and she felt the warm wetness of his tears dampening her hair.

He said "I remember how terrified I was of losing you. I'd finally found my mate and almost lost you. It's not just that. I make decisions for the town, and its people, yes, but I *know* many of them, and they accept my role. What I just did was make a decision for a person that I simply *don't know* the same way. Is hard, making such decisions outside of battle. In battle, it is you against them. Often, to live, you must decide to kill them. This is no fight. This is someone I hope can help us. I do not want to hurt the Beast in *any* way."

Gyada saw the two beings that had been responsible for caging her walk up with what looked like a black square cut rock with a glowing gem on the top. They talked to each other in the language which she was slowly learning, but she couldn't comprehend exactly what they were saying. She was shocked when she saw the man push the gem into the black box. She had a sudden burst of buzzing in her head, and slowly, exhaustion crept into her bones. Her last thought before unconsciousness took her, was that these beings weren't human. They had mastered the technology of the being that had changed her and had found a way to kill her without violence.

It had been just over two hours when the intercom that had been set up throughout the cave system called them back to the cage. Apparently, not only had the beast woken up but to everyone's surprise except Janna's it had managed to change into its human form ... that of a woman. TOM and ADAM must have failed to tell Boris that the beast was female. At least based on his reaction to the announcement of her form. Boris released Janna and rushed down to the creature's cage. Janna followed as closely as she could behind him.

Maybe now they would get the answers they wanted.

Gyada was surprised to wake up again. She had felt

oblivion take her, and had been sure that finally she would be allowed to die. Clearly, it had not been time for the Valkyrie to take her, nor had her captors been trying to kill her.

She kept still with her eyes closed as she tried to think through what had happened. What had they been trying to do? She spent a while thinking on what they might have wanted. Her body didn't feel different, but something about herself did. She spent more time trying to puzzle out what it could be. Eventually, out of other ideas, she decided to attempt to take her human form as she did from time to time.

Suddenly, she could feel her bare skin against the rough, rock floor of the cave. It had worked! For the first time in what it seemed like an eternity, she had skin, fingers, feet, no fur and no claws. She breathed in a shuddering breath of relief, overcome with a sense of wonder, joy, and solace, she started sobbing uncontrollably.

It was then that Janna hurried into the room. Gyada shuffled back from the tall, imposing woman. It wasn't that she was ashamed of her nudity, but rather a spike of fear. This young woman had assisted in taking her down in her more fearsome form. She had no doubt in this weaker form she was similarly outmatched. Janna put a bundle down in front of her cage. She said, "I thought you might like these, come now put them on," in a calm, soothing voice. Gyada simply backed away a little further and shook her head, having no idea what Janna had said. Janna sighed, picked up the top, shook it out and pointed one finger at the top then at Gyada. Slowly the wild woman moved forward, approaching the fabric as if it was magic. Tentatively she touched it, then ran her hand down the fabric that was far softer than any she had touched before. This was fabric that might even be finer than any she had seen a noble wear.

She lightly gripped it, and Janna let it drop. Boris had wanted to come in with Janna, but Janna had refused. Quite wisely it seemed, now given how skittish this person was in her human form. Two people in the room with her may have overwhelmed her and made communication even harder. Especially since they apparently shared no common tongue as Janna had run through greetings in every language she knew.

What they had here was a person unsettled by their surroundings, scared by the unfamiliarity of everything around her. Eventually, Janna got Gyada into her clothes, although she had refused the underwear. The buttons had also been a problem, as for whatever reason, her fingers were clumsy despite being only slightly bulkier than the average woman's. Once she had Gyada calm again after getting her dressed, Janna led her out of the cage and over to a small table. The table had a tray with a large bowl of food, water cup, and a loaf of bread.

Boris had quietly slipped in and sat down next to Janna, putting his arm around her and just looked at Gyada. Fortunately, the smells of the food had Gyada completely distracted and unconcerned when he did so.

Janna pointed out how to use cutlery to Gyada, but Boris lightly touched a hand and shook his head. It was entirely likely, given that she was multiple centuries old, that she had never eaten with cutlery before. She ate somewhat clumsily and with haste, leaving quite a mess by the end of the meal. Her face went bright red when she saw how much food had fallen off her plate, but both Janna and Boris just smiled and shook their heads at her. After the meal had been finished, Janna led Gyada to a room that Boris had told a sergeant to relinquish.

When the sergeant had found out why, there had been no complaints.

CHAPTER EIGHT

Gyada went into a room with a raised sleeping mat, thicker than any she had experienced. With everything that had happened in the last few hours, she still felt very tired. When she lay on the mat, she found it more comfortable than she had used, including anything when she had been human before.

Soon, sleep overcame her.

The next few days were very frustrating for Boris and Janna as they sought to communicate with the woman who had been the Beast. It had taken two days to explain names and identify themselves to her. It was as if she had lost something of the concepts of being human and was slowly rediscovering them over the first week.

Their breakthrough came when they passed Shen practicing Kurtherian with TOM. She started speaking to them slowly and awkwardly in that strange language, as she was unused to speaking to anyone anymore. Eventually, they got her history from using that language.

TOM was amazed at how fluent her understanding of

Kurtherian was, even if her Kurtherian speech was slow and methodical at best. Over the following weeks between TOM and Shen, they managed to teach her the basics of Russian and English.

She stubbornly refused to tell either of them of her past stating that it would be disrespectful to their leaders. When asked who she believed they were, she pointed to Boris and Janna. Everyone had smiled when they heard that.

She would be in for a bigger shock when or if she finally met Bethany Anne. She had identified the leaders of this base, so it could be said at least she hadn't lost an understanding of human leadership roles. When she wasn't practicing the language with TOM and Shen, Janna familiarized her with modern amenities. Although she still refused to wear a bra, complaining that they were torture devices, she did take to wearing other undergarments.

Boris busied himself continuing the setup of the defenses of the town, and the training of the men and women with weapons. They drilled in the responses they should take in an emergency. He insisted that everyone in the town should at least know how to fire a weapon, both rifle and handgun. He would not have a town under his protection be such an easy target again.

Gyada was unsettled by the fact that she could no longer hear the voice that had been her constant companion for centuries. She was now without that companion. Janna suggested that perhaps a young Were at her side would aid her. Allow her to adjust to this new and confusing world. Help her find a feeling of balance and purpose.

. . .

Moscow, Office of the Department of Settlements, Russia

"So, you called me here, Evgenni. Pulled me out just as the first buildings of my new settlement are going up. What the fuck is going on you son-of-a-bitch? We had an agreement. I could choose two places to settle my people from existing NVG bases. There was *no* restriction on this, yes? With how many decided to stay away we decided only one." Boris glared at the political appointee. Evgenni was sweating heavily, despite the cool in the room they were in.

"Boris, this is not the agreement we made. The agreement was you take over any two bases that the NVG had held in Siberia and settle there." Evgenni responded in a calm tone despite the obvious fear he held for Boris. Through the sweat and the light fidgeting, he was actually holding up extremely well. "I am sure that some sort of arrangement involving military personnel assisting in the security of..."

"*Yob tvoyu mat'!* Evgenni, you stupid son of a bitch. I will not risk having my people killed on political orders after what they have already been through. Do you understand *pizdyonysh*? The government did nothing... *NOTHING*... To protect my people when the NVG went after them the first time. The military was involved in attacking them." Evgenni's face was steadily getting redder as Boris continued, and he opened his mouth to interrupt. Boris raised a hand to forestall any comment. "You let a *proklyatyh nemeckih fashistov...* German neo-Nazi... gain an incredible amount of influence and power within and without our military, and you expect me to sit here and accept you putting military forces amongst the people I protect? *Nyet.* I will support the government as I can, but my people have been through enough. Hell, for all I care you can deny the military's protection if someone externally decides to target the town." Boris sneered at the political appointee.

"Boris, please, it is not the time of the Reds. We do not kill people out of hand. They're not looking for traitors in the way the Reds did. Your people are loyal children of the Motherland. We simply wish to be more involved in case someone does go after you."

"No, Evgenni. You keep pushing, I'll bring Bethany Anne into these discussions." The bureaucrat's eyes went wide, and face went white at the mention of Boris' Czarina. Evidently, word about her had penetrated the Russian bureaucracies. "Part of the reason I cannot allow what you suggest is that Bethany Anne will be providing us additional support in protecting the town. It will also enable us to be available to assist the government should any... *unusual*... Problems pop up again." Evgenni's shoulders stiffened significantly at the mention of "unusual problems."

Boris continued, "But to deal with these unusual problems, we need freedom from government interference. Many of the actions we will need to take will be somewhat... Grey. It is, therefore, better for everyone for the government to not have to acknowledge that they even occurred. If the military notices comings and goings of certain people from there, eventually someone who doesn't need to know will connect those movements with events in other regions of Russia."

"Boris, I am under orders here. I need to get something out of this, or I may as well throw away not only my career but my family's well-being." A look of hopelessness crossed Evgenni's face. "Please, isn't there something you can do?"

Boris thought about that for a minute. There were actually several things he could do. "I will make an offer to you, and provide something of interest for the government. We are getting housing delivered manufactured from the leftovers of the space mining operations. Basically, solid formed rock walls that can be fitted together to make a house. I will ask Bethany Anne to also provide the government with several samples of this material and make it available for the Russian government to purchase upon request at a discounted price."

Evgenni twitched nervously in his seat, "And you offer for me?"

Boris smiled. "You're a brave man Evgenni. Not many would have the balls to face me down like you have. So I offer you this." Boris pulled a pair of radio transmitters from his pocket. "If your family and yourself find others harassing you, contact me through these. We'll reach you far faster than anyone could imagine. And we will offer you a place in our community. If you choose to assist me by giving me further information of any rumblings against our town that would be welcome, but my offer of assistance to you in troubling situations is not contingent upon it. It is only contingent upon you convincing the government that the deal I am offering now is the best one they will find provided by me and Bethany Anne. Understood?"

There was a wave of gratitude and relief across Evgenni's face. "Thank you." He sighed "I know you're trying to do your best to be fair, Boris. But we are all caught between rocks and hard places these days."

Boris nodded and shook Evgenni's hand. Those radio transmitters were only slightly different from standard. Even if Evgenni handed them over to the government, there wasn't anything Bethany Anne objected to governments having involved in their technology or manufacture. It was well worth the risk of the Russians getting a hold of them for the potential of future early warnings of problems from that same government.

Besides, Boris had to wonder why Evgenni had been chosen to be the government's emissary. No one was ever chosen to be an emissary to him for nice reasons.

CHAPTER NINE

New Romanovka , Archangelsk, Russia.

Boris dreaded the day that Frank turned up. He would be obsessed with getting the details of her life before Gyada had been trapped in the cave, although she would be reticent about it from what he had seen. Boris wasn't sure if it was because she didn't remember it, or if it was because it was painful for her to remember.

To say Bethany Anne was frustrated with Boris' slow progress in both deciphering the Beast, and extracting information from the computer would be an understatement. Every report he'd sent her for months had said, "We need more time" and Bethany Anne was not a patient person. After the first month, Boris had handed the task of daily reporting to Janna, because Boris was sick of hearing frustration in his Tsarina's voice that he fully understood and could not fault.

But he could also do nothing about.

Finally, after she had felt confident enough in her Russian to fully explain her story, Boris had sent a report which had taken some of the stress from both Janna and himself. Boris even suggested that Marcus and TOM question her knowledge to see if she might be able to aid them. Both with insights about the unknown alien and to test what knowledge the AI had taught her in its boredom. She had already shown a quick adaptation to several items that were far beyond the era she was from as if something was finally clicking in her mind.

TOM had been enthusiastic about the idea, Marcus less so. He grumbled about damned theoreticians not having enough real-world knowledge to understand the problems. Bethany Anne had slowly worn him down on the issue. After all, what was the harm in having another person who understood the theories in detail to bounce ideas off of?

Gyada expressed some concerns about being shifted off to passive work. She had been confined for so long she wanted to get out of there. See what the world was now like. Go further, see the stars if she could. She had slowly come to understand the possibilities of her acquired knowledge as she had been taught the last century's history. More so once she had talked to Marcus and Team BMW.

Gyada's restlessness and impatience hindered her integration into the modern world and the town. People found it uncomfortable to work with her for any length of time due to the constant fidgeting and obvious desire to be doing something more active or outdoorsy.

None of the command group were comfortable with throwing her straight into the militia training programs. They had no idea how controlled she was, and any Were who lacked iron control was a risk to those they trained with, especially humans.

So Boris set aside a part of every morning for her to train with him and either Janna or Danislav and three of the wolves. At least it started out as three of the wolves.

Training one-on-one with her in human form, she was an even match with Danislav although she could sometimes manage to take down two of his friends. The form her hand-to-hand fighting took involved getting in close. She was a small woman, so focused on throwing and grappling them. All in all, it was a wise choice for a smaller opponent against a larger. With everyone involved being Were, there was no way she could have taken them punch for punch. After a few days, male competitors started wearing cups regularly. She had no qualms about going for vulnerable places.

When one of them complained about it to Boris, he'd raised an eyebrow at her, getting her to answer. "Stop whining like a baby. If you are unprepared by training for what might happen in combat, you won't be ready for it when it occurs."

And they looked at Boris with slightly pleading expression, he'd shrugged and told them, "What she said. There is nothing wrong with her using such moves. As long as she doesn't try to break a neck or back, I'm a happy man."

Fighting in their other forms, however, was a different matter.

Gyada stood inside a circle of the wolves the first day. They snarled and snapped in an attempt to unnerve her. Her form was much smaller than most of the werebears the Weres had encountered. Their overconfidence showed when the first one charged in only to be grabbed by the scruff of the neck by Gyada's mouth and thrown across the room with a yelp. There was a solid cracking sound when one of its legs hit the wall. Even with the Weres ability to heal fast, that Wolf would be out of this fight.

The three remaining wolves started circling back and forth. Their goal was to make her lose track of one of them so that one could dart in and hamstring her. To say it was a spectacular failure was an understatement. She managed to toss the one that tried to hamstring her against a wall with a remarkably dexterous twist of her back paw. Gyada then grabbed the one that had feinted to distract her by the scruff of the neck and threw him into the third.

She moved that little bit faster than they were expecting, catching them off guard. She wasn't quite as fast as Boris and Janna, but she was faster than the average werewolf. Once they changed back, she scolded them for hesitating. For thinking too much before attacking.

She still didn't seem to recognize how much the world has changed. Her companion, a lithe Mongolian female Were called Nergui, was the one who suggested they run her through rifle and pistol training with a group of normal humans. Paul had been reluctant to allow it, but eventually caved in when it was pointed out to him that she was no more a danger to the other human trainees than they were to each other.

Paul ripped a gun from the hands of one of the other trainees within a couple of minutes of handing them out, for failure to follow the order to keep the muzzle pointed away from everyone, preferably towards the ground. He raised the gun and it barked as a shot fired from it.

"First thing when you get a gun, check the damned thing doesn't have a bullet in the chamber before you do anything. When it is first handed to you, check that it is unloaded. Even once you've checked don't point towards something you don't wanna destroy. Got it kiddies?" Murmurs of agreement had followed. Considering some in the group were definitely older than Paul, Gyada found this amusing, but she made sure that she followed his instructions. It was evident he'd trained people with these weapons before.

When she saw how much destruction even the smaller 'pistol' did she was significantly more cautious about everything around her. She also stopped being so focused on being allowed to roam. It was clear that they were worried about her being injured by something she simply hadn't seen as a threat.

She is also unsure why those guns that had fired at her earlier hadn't done more damage to her. After all, Boris and Janna had no problems tearing her flesh with their claws when they trained with her. It was a question, but not one that needed a quick answer. Despite everything, she felt the guns were an inappropriate tool of war.

They offended her sensibilities.

Philosophically, she seemed to consider guns cheating. War was brutal, and she'd let slip that she had been a shield maiden amongst the Rus. In her opinion, they were items for pure destruction, not suitable for honorable warfare. She had no objections to archery, and even crossbows were grudgingly acceptable as real weapons of war, but on some level, guns were killing machines used by the masses.

Perhaps it was the relative lack of skill required to

become proficient with them. Gyada had spent years learning how to use a sword, axe, and shield properly in warfare. The basics of learning how to use a gun took minutes. And in some ways she was correct. The weapons massively increased the number of people able to be put on a frontline, as soldiers no longer had to be trained for years on end and supported by a large population base. They could be conscripted and given a few weeks training, then sent to the battlefront.

Gyada's considered opinion appeared to be that the clashing of the massive armies of the twentieth century in World War I and World War II were simply a crude attempt at population control. She could respect the skill of individual generals in outmaneuvering and outthinking their enemies. All she saw in such massive forces was the pointless sacrifices of many lives. From a certain point of view, Boris could see her point. It wasn't unlike Bethany Anne's methods. Bethany Anne didn't focus on using large forces. She focused on training the best small forces she could.

With the speed, strength, and skill that a Were or a vampire could bring to bear, each individual of her rather smaller forces could probably take on a company of ordinary soldiers. They were trained to the level of special forces and had additional enhancements that were force multipliers beyond that.

Something didn't quite mesh here for either Janna or Shen.

Yes, Gyada had literally centuries to consider consequences, but why would a late Dark Age person consider such things? How would she have thought about the concept of it initially? They wondered what was in the Kurtherian computer's database and what it had taught her beyond her understanding of the Etheric. Marcus had described her theoretical understanding of Gravitics as exceptional.

What else, they wondered, had she learned?

CHAPTER TEN

Gyada's Past

Finally, Gyada felt that she had a good enough grasp on Russian and English between them to talk to them about her past with minimal interruptions for clarity. If she didn't know the right wording in one language, she would switch to the other

"I was born, oh, I am not really sure how long ago. Shen has suggested somewhere between eight and nine centuries. It was in the country you now call Sweden, what was then called Svitjod. My father was a renowned warrior, a wearer of the bear shirt. I was his third daughter, though he had six sons. All of us were raised as warriors, as befit the get of the champion of the King of Svitjold." Her tone slowly changed to a rhythmic and melodic cadence as she spoke, as if letting the story tell itself.

"Children of my father, and his father before him had an ax placed in their hands before they took the first milk from their mother's breast. Some say his line could trace itself back to Tyr, although he never claimed that. He simply focused on making sure his children carried on the legacy of skill and loyalty to their leaders. He had maintained and strengthened in his father's name. He expected the same from us."

"A tale reached us from the Finns, who our then-King had friendly contact with. It was about a land beyond theirs. This land had been a prosperous kingdom, but when its ruler died his eight sons fell to squabbling over who was best to take his place. This had resulted in a conflict that lasted many years and stripped the kingdom of warriors. Now, the King of the Finns was a wise man. He felt that with only one son to come after him, annexing that kingdom would stretch his resources to the point it would make his nation vulnerable."

"My King had two sons, both highly capable. Both wished the glory of conquering and ruling a new kingdom. However, in the end, it was decided the eldest should go. The youngest already had a wife and a son, and was the preferred heir of his father for the stability that gave his future rule."

"My father was getting on in years, and this campaign would enable him to secure the future of our family. Thus, my eldest brother was chosen to replace him as champion, and the rest of the family followed our father into the war."

"Our force numbered in the thousands, with adventurers, poor freemen and former thralls joining our ranks. However, once we reached the lands we were to conquer we found a problem. There were no large bodies of troops to face us, only small harassing forces. But the King's eldest son had been a wise man too. He declared that each man would choose to form warbands around a single leader, who he would name Jarl. Each Jarl was responsible for declaring the borders and eliminating any who objected to their rule within their lands. Fully half the warriors decided to stay under the King, some of these being younger sons of Jarls from the homeland, but the majority were freed thralls and townsfolk hoping to prosper in this new land. The losing natives would be slaves to aid their enterprises and crafts."

"It was a fine land we found ourselves in, with large flat areas suitable for growing grains. My father and his youngest son and I all joined the same warband, ostensibly under Firi, the youngest of my brothers. My father did not wish to erode the legitimacy of any of his sons. By refusing to take the title of leader and Jarl in the new land, he prevented this. By aiding his youngest, most saw him giving the wisdom of experience to the son who needed it most. He was old, and I think saw his last chance to die in battle. He was saddened by the thought of not dying on the field of battle he loved so much. It was with joy, not sadness that we found ourselves engaged by perhaps the largest of the former ruler's remaining factions. It was a battle in which we were outnumbered, though not by a large amount."

"We formed shield walls and moved towards each other, as this is how our battles were fought in that time. Axes were rapped against our shields to keep the movement pace. But my father saw an opportunity, dropped his shield and called for his great ax. He charged the enemy alone. The impact of his body into the opposing shield wall was heard across two fields. The impact had cracked the two enemy shields his body hit, allowing him to penetrate the formation and forcing it to slow. An enemy soldier was thrown into the shield wall from the inside by a mighty swing of my father's ax, forcing the formation to slow further and disrupting their planned movement."

"Our group quickened its pace. Moving at a rolling speed, we slammed into the hampered formation."

"When we collided with the enemy shield wall, it crumbled. Three others and I found ourselves surrounded for a short time by the enemies. Two of my companions attempted to flee back to the safety of our main group but were cut down. The remaining man and I fought back-to-back keeping several of the enemy away until our shield wall reached us. That day, I found my husband."

"After that battle, and after we had buried the dead, which included my father, the time came to split the land for the freeholds. What was the Jarl's alone, and what was given to others for service in the Jarl's forces. What was to be held free of the Jarl. Before the land was split, I declared my intention to marry, and my brother gave his blessing. Therefore, myself and my future husband were given a freehold, as were many of the warriors who fought in that battle. My new husband and I shared a patch that was larger than the grants to individual fighters. Some objected though the grant was smaller than any other two warrior's grants."

"The original holding's borders are not more than thirty kilometers from where we sit today."

"I was happy for many years with my husband and bore him four children, one son and three daughters. We were happy until he was killed in revenge raid against the Sami tribespeople to the north. Then trouble started occurring.

None of my children were old enough to be fully trained in the warrior's arts. Many, especially from the local population, thought I could not hold the former lands without him. Our holding was on the border so that we were obligated to protect our lands and to watch the border for the Jarl. That placement left us without his easy support. The distance became known along with the fact my husband was dead. Many raiders thought to take advantage of this. That was despite my reputation as a shieldmaiden of great skill, one to be feared on any battlefield. I was successful in defending the holding, but suffered grave losses."

"I was captured by the strange alien with my children as we started on a Yule trip to my brother's hold. Partly to celebrate with family, and so my children could meet their cousins. Partly to ask him for aid. It pointed one of its devices at me, and I crashed to the ground, shrieking in agony. When I could move again, it pointed it threateningly at my children and told us to follow. What choice was there for us?"

"For some time, the creature was only interested in tormenting me. What it did to me, the pain it caused I cannot and will not describe. It kept assuring me it was improving me, and eventually showed me how to change my form into the other one you have seen. I was content at this time. My children were not harmed, were healthy, and fed with food the creature provided and deer I hunted. It only seemed interested in me."

"Then it started doing things to my children. I felt true despair and began searching for a way to, if not free us all, free them from its control. We were not slaves. We were not thralls. We were proud descendants of a Jarl's line.

That it treated us all as slaves, that it hurt my children..."
She broke off, sobs wracking her body. Janna moved close
to comfort her, but Gyada shook her head.

She wiped the tears from her face, "I found a way to
allow my children to escape. The being did not need sleep,
not like humans do, but I learned to recognize the signs of
when it wasn't paying attention to the world around us.
During one of those periods I changed, broke my children
free of their chains, and told them to run far and fast. To
change to the forms that had been inflicted upon them and
use those forms to aid in their escape. And never to look
back. To warn their children, and their children's children,
that this area was too dangerous to return to."

"When the creature woke up, it took some time to learn
my children were no longer there. It started ranting that it
would catch them, bring them back, and cause me pain
until I broke, and would become obedient to its wishes. I
shifted and charged it, moving faster than I ever had ever
attempted. It seemed to be in shock, and the blows from
my paws interrupted it as it tried to yell something out."

Her listeners were now captivated for various reasons
by her tale. Boris because he realized this may well be his
ancestor telling him the story of how his people were
created. Janna because of the loss the woman had faced.
Shen and Alecta were both fascinated by the technologies
she was describing.

"I found myself unable to return to my human shape. I
was in despair. I hoped that there was some way that my
brother's village would take me in, so I traveled there. They
tried to chase me off with fire and sword. When the first
blade bit my skin, it was as if the Beast took over. The

anger of the betrayal added to my rage, for I had traveled by my homestead first and scented that nobody had investigated the fact that I had not arrived when I had sent messages ahead of my imminent arrival."

"I am ashamed to admit that I left the village without another living creature in it. That I ate the flesh of many that I killed there that winter. My rage that nothing had been done to avenge my capture burned strong at the time. I continued to raid my other brother's holdings over the next few years until finally I was hunted by a man with strength beyond my own. With strength beyond anything that I had ever encountered. I then retreated back to the cave, making brief forays out to hunt for food, then returning. But that powerful man tracked me down. He cornered me in the cave, and I was certain it was my time for Valhalla. There would be worse ways to go than being killed by this great warrior."

"Instead he showed me a kind of mercy. I do not know if he realized I would survive as long as I have, but rather than kill me he collapsed the entrance to the cave. It happened to be the only entrance to the cave that I could use in my animal form to escape."

"In my time within the cave, a voice talked to me. At first, I thought it had been some sort of spirit sent to punish me. Eventually, I came to realize that it was trapped the same as me. I learned many things from it. Learned of wonders I never thought I might have the opportunity to see." Her eyes glittered for a moment as if there was something she desperately wanted but was still not sure she could achieve.

"I couldn't know how long had passed when I finally

found my way back out of the cave. I was also much calmer, having realized that seeing my animal form would have terrified many normal humans. I did my best to limit those I killed outside the caves to those who sought to harm me."

She looked up, "And so here we are." Gyada finished the story, showing a mixture of relief and exhaustion. Relief from finally telling someone what had happened to her, finally being able to give these people who had treated her with kindness, her past. Exhaustion from going through her memories, with so much pain in them.

Boris and Janna looked at each other. It seemed likely that whatever the alien had shouted had activated something that had rewritten the critical portion of the nanites code for changing forms. That explained the section that TOM and ADAM had found garbled.

Finally, Boris felt they had enough information to conclude that she was remarkably adaptable. When taking into account the time she had spent alone, or at least only in contact with an AI of questionable sanity, he had to conclude that she was as sane as anyone else in the group he'd met. They all had their quirks. They all had things they kept hidden.

New Romonavka, Celebration of the Second Battle of Romonavka

"... So I found myself in command of the entire force and had no idea if Boris was alive." Danislav said. "Boris had made me second in command the night before. I wasn't sure I was his best choice for the role, but it had to be someone who wasn't in his bunker. I thought Paul would have been a better choice and would have been better out of the bunker." There was a murmur from the old hands. "Boris pointed out that Paul might be a great XO, hell even a great small unit commander, but with his luck, no sane person would put him in command of an entire operation." Laughter traveled around the room as the old hands thought on the number of situations Paul had gotten himself into, and somehow out of. Paul saluted Danislav with a beer in his hand and a grin on his face.

"Still and all, we had a good killing that day. We had the enemy outflanked, and although they had light armored vehicles, the tactics we used restricted its utility. The worst they managed to do to us was take out Boris' bunker, and that was more a case of luck than anything. Encircling them and taking out their vehicles probably got rid of a quarter to a third of the NVG's forces at the time. Nothing more than the *svlotsky* deserved. We got to hammer them for our dead and what they tried to do to our town and to Mother Russia." A cheer went up, and glasses clinked in a toast to the Motherland.

The crowd then broke into smaller groups, talking about individual actions. Boris directed an intense gaze on Janna. She had never told the story of what had actually happened in the bunker, not even to him. He felt it would be a good tale, one that could give people a good example of Murphy's Law. Not that Danislav hadn't shown that in his story.

His tale was a better example of how proper planning prevents piss poor performance, though.

It also might be a good way to get Gyada accepted and out of her shell socially. She didn't talk about her past or what it had been like 'back in the day.' None of the tales from that day of battle had gotten her to loosen up any either, although she had perked up at the story of a bayonet charge on a small group of shaken NVG around a troop truck.

She finally displayed an interest when the descriptions turned to close in, hand-to-hand combat. She talked to the man who brought up the incident for a bit, discussing the tactics and movements used in bayonet drill. Boris overheard Gyada saying that from the description it was somewhat similar to those used in short spear fighting.

Finally, Boris rolled his eyes at Janna. She looked at him angrily. The anger wasn't directed so much at him, like the fact that she knew that one way or another the story would become a tale to be told at every future anniversary, either by her or by someone else.

It would become a legend, a part of the history of the region, the conflict and her. She moved quietly to the center of the room, and Danislav saw her. Catching Boris' eye, he raised his arms and yelled, "Quiet, a new story is to be told."

Janna flinched slightly and glared at him with some heat. She'd hoped for the noise to cover some of the story. Still, she started with, "There was a blast, and the entire front of the bunker disappeared, and everything went black. When I came to, I'd been thrown against one of the shelter walls. I found myself acting automatically, checking for possible survivors."

The mercs and ex-military in the room nodded unconsciously at that. It was their training if physically able and taking no fire to check for casualties after an explosion. And with the bunker half collapsed, like everyone in the room knew from previous stories, she wasn't taking fire.

She continued "Paul had a strong pulse, and his arm still moved. No external wounds and there was fuck all I could do about any internal bleeding or damaged organs. Above my skills. So I turned to Boris. He still had a weak pulse, but I couldn't see him breathing. What I could see was a four-foot splinter from the bunker wall pinning him to the chair. It was at least six inches at the base..." As she delved more deeply into the telling of the story her fears from the event left her and she became more animated and portrayed it with strength and vividness.

"... Waking up looking like a famine victim was one of the more unpleasant experiences I've had." Janna concluded the story of how she had saved Boris and unintentionally initiated the change to a werebear. She knew the cost, the other prices she was still paying. The last thing she would do is encourage people by telling them that it wouldn't be that way for someone else.

Boris approved and his gaze settled on each and every Were in the room. None here knew both his and Janna's nanites had been modified to prevent that happening again. Nor did they need to know.

For once, even Paul kept his mouth shut.

"'Tis a lesson to learn in the story, too. That Changing someone isn't something done lightly." Boris said in a hushed tone, the memory of his close miss clear on his face. It was obvious to everyone in the room how much nearly losing Janna still haunted him. "It has a price, like everything else, and the price can be the death of someone. We will do our best to prevent unnecessary deaths, we have things that might help. But there is no 'Silver Bullet' that guarantees a fix here. People will die if we Weres aren't careful when, who, and where we try to change someone. Understood?"

A murmur traveled the room. Heads nodded, both Were and unmodified human. It was clear that the lesson had gone home... and that there was now a better understanding of the price many had paid over the centuries. A price forged from love more often than not, but a steep price at that.

Faraday Cage, Beast Caves, Russia

It was a simple question that triggered the breakthrough that they needed on what the hell had happened at this location. Why a Kurtherian had crashed here after (based on the nature of Gyada's transformation) having traveled to other locations on the planet.

Gyada asked, "Why can't I hear her voice anymore? I thought she'd just gone quiet, resting, thinking or afraid for a while, but this is far longer than she's been silent before." She paused "I think it is a 'her' at least. It's hard to tell." She grinned a bit impishly. "From what I've learned I was trapped for eight centuries. It didn't *seem* that long to me, but to be honest, I think I just let time flow around me. Some of what she taught me was fascinating," a look of wonder crossed her face, "and I may have lost track of how long we were talking. I still find it hard to believe any race with the knowledge can cross space, see other worlds. But with what I've seen that we as a species have achieved while I was... away, I am starting to understand."

Paul looked confused and asked "Waddya mean? We weren't gettin' anywhere with stuff in space really until Bethany Anne and TOM got together."

Alecta punched him in the shoulder and said "We went from pounding metal to getting objects to the outer solar system in the period she's talking about. Sometimes I wonder why I married you when you act like such an imbecile."

"I thought we agreed that you were going to restrict your insults about me to two syllables, dear," Paul answered with a barely hidden grin. Alecta spun around and threw up her arms muttering in Russian. Once her back was turned, Paul's grin broke out wide.

Everyone else in the room smiled at him when she wasn't facing them. A throat cleared at the corner of the chamber. Well almost everyone. Boris was standing at the back of the room with a thoughtful scowl on his face.

"What did you mean, she stopped talking to you?" He had the expression of someone going down Alice's rabbit hole... and not liking the experience one bit. "When did this happen?"

Gyada looked thoughtful, her eyes flashing back and forth. "Twelve, maybe thirteen days after you captured me, I think." Boris looked at Shen and Janna.

"That was when you got the Faraday cage up and running, right?" Boris asked.

Shen mutely nodded, and Janna answered, "Yes. It was also when the cursed whispering stopped, and I managed a good night's sleep for the first time in more than three weeks."

She looked at him, appraising his mood. "It's got a fair amount of room inside, and a chair is already there..."

She cut off as Boris raised his hand. "No, love. This is my responsibility. Therefore, my risk. If someone has to go into the cage, it'll be me."

Gyada looked up sharply and asked, "What are you talking about? By the nine realms, *what* is a Faraday cage?"

Shen quirked an eyebrow, then answered. "It's a metal net or lattice surrounding an object that has electricity running through it ..."

Gyada finished for him "That blocks certain wavelengths of the Electromagnetic spectrum, yes, yes. I just hadn't heard it called that befo..." and she stopped dead. "You mean it's been communicating with me by *radio waves* all these centuries? And how come the signal wasn't detected..." her eyes narrowed in thought "Must be a lot of metal ores in the cave walls, blocking the frequencies it uses." she mused.

She'd come to the same conclusion in minutes that had taken an hour for Shen, Janna, and Boris to reach with just a couple of pieces of information.

It was a little odd to see her work through a problem. It was almost like a person was there just as a thesaurus, dictionary, and wall for her ideas to bounce off. "Well, I can tell you she won't be happy. She doesn't like boredom. That's why she taught me so many things. Teaching a primitive like me was a challenge. I'd better go in with anyone that wants to try to talk to her."

She looked at Boris and Janna. "How's your Kurtherian?"

They glanced at each other and shrugged, "It's not." Boris answered for both of them. "We haven't had time to learn a language since everything came unglued."

"Well, Hel and Niflheim. I don't know if you're going to be able to talk to her then. She taught me that first up. She doesn't like other languages."

"She'll need to learn Russian at least. Probably English

as well. If she doesn't talk to Bethany Anne, the decision might be made to simply take her apart."

Gyada frowned but slowly nodded. If the voice from her head wouldn't associate with whoever was guarding it, the safest solution would be to simply dismantle the box that held her. Then she wouldn't attract unwanted attention nor would she be a potential threat to her guardians.

CHAPTER TWELVE

<u>Moscow, Chinese Intelligence Outpost, Russia.</u>

Li Chen-Wu was an unhappy man. Werecat. Whatever. The elders of the clan had tasked him to find out where the Ghost Bear had relocated. To do that he had to possibly burn one of their best resources for information in Russia. One of the senior spies at this intelligence outpost.

Yes, the man was human, just another readily bribed Communist party member. But he was very effective at his job, more than willing to pass on information, and Li Chen-wu liked him. He also didn't like having to expend assets he actually personally got along with.

There weren't many of them after all.

"Bohai, what do you have for me? We gave you a name, and that he was likely involved in the recent disturbances inside Russia." Li asked somewhat impatiently. The shorter he kept this, the less risk there was to both him and Bohai. Li definitely didn't want to be in the Ghost Bear's reach while he was alone in Russia. If they could infiltrate forces to his location and stage an attack, that would be a different matter. Li didn't care how powerful a Were was, there was no chance that a single Were could hold off several of the clan's elites.

Bohai bowed deeply, and replied with, "It's good to see you too, Li. How's the family? Everything going well for your clan? It would be unfortunate if something would happen to you while you are so far from any help they could offer."

Li glared at Bohai. "You wouldn't dare. Besides, this may well be a case where you can gain prestige by setting one of the official enemies of the party against another."

"Yes, there is that," Bohai answered. "After all it is clear there are links between this Boris and the Bitch Queen that flattened those mountains in eastern China. But I just wanted to remind you, that payment is due." A vicious grin erupted on his face, and he continued, "I have reports of your clan's weaknesses and now, I fear you less. Still, that is no reason we cannot work together. At least when our goals align. But you must think me a complete fool if I didn't do more research on your people considering everything that has happened."

Li nodded and hid an internal grimace.

The problem with truly effective agents was that they had to be intelligent. Otherwise, they weren't worth the effort to nurture and maintain. Bohai was one of the most intelligent agents. He'd always been cautious in his dealings with the Sacred Clan.

It had been as much fear as money that kept him in line. That the fear was now a reduced factor in his thinking was a problem. It was almost as if he expected to start shifting their arrangements, so it was of more benefit to him personally. Possibly turning the relationship into a detriment to the clans as a whole.

That was a problem for another day.

The issue could not be forgotten, but the bigger problem facing the clan was a possibility of not only the technology slipping through their fingers but landing in the hands of an enemy.

"You're fortunate that I have managed to suborn a member of the directorate of municipalities. It seems that one very unusual town has been set up very recently under the Siberian resettlement program." He raised an eyebrow at Li.

"Yes, yes I know, the program to expand Siberia's population base by resettling poor Russians and foreigners in Eastern Siberia. Adding to the population there and developing Russia's economy as a whole."

"Yes, well one of the new settlements under that program is in a very unusual location. Its name is also, shall we say, inpolitick in the current climate in Russia. New Romanovka." Bohai tapped a folder on the desk before he threw it to Li. "You never asked for this before, but considering what you're facing I thought it rude if nothing else not to give you all the information I had available on the individuals involved."

The folder was titled 'Boris' and Li quickly started flipping through the voluminous data. When he reached a section dating to World War Two, he found something that confirmed Boris was who they were looking for.

Soviet Wartime records showing a codename 'Ghost Bear'. It seems that Boris had been responsible for disrupting David's influence over the Weres, whoever

David was. He followed that to the footnote. 'David, supposedly a brother of Peter, supposed child of Michael.'

It seemed that the UnknownWorld was not as unknown as the Sacred Clan or, supposedly, Peter and Michael would have preferred.

"Where did you get this information, Bohai? If I didn't like you, this information would be a death sentence, one that I would have to carry out immediately." Li said in tones that showed his seriousness. "To keep my leaders happy I will have to find someone to kill for this information being available to you. Tell me."

"The intelligence directorate has always collected myths and legends. It's better to have a collection of them on hand in case they turn out to be true after all. I merely pieced together what was out there. So there is no one you need to kill, Li. You did not have access to the information, and I pieced together what you might be asking about." He pointed at the folder, "Few in the directorate would risk writing a report like that. To rely on myths and legend, then transpose it across known facts, that is too far outside the box for the directorate's leaders to find acceptable. This report was written on a private computer that has never been connected to the Internet. You do not have to worry about others seeing it. And I will still be useful to you."

Li ignored that and quickly moved forward, grasping Bohai by the neck. As he did, he felt the barrel of a shotgun pressed against his belly. "Let go or a load of silver shot will be where your chest is now. I told you I do my research. If I didn't believe we could come to an understanding, I wouldn't have turned up for this meeting. I believe we can. I even may have a way for you to infiltrate Clan members into Siberia. What they do from there is up to you and your leaders. But if I have to kill you then a lot of wasted effort has gone into this. And if you kill me you'll never get that information. I believe we are in what is classically called a 'stand-off,' old friend."

Li started to tighten his grip on Bohai's neck. He felt the man's hand twitching and thought better of it. A double load of silver from any shotgun shell would probably be lethal.

That would leave two dead, one with a strange reaction to silver and a report on a third, in which there was a claim he was sensitive to silver. Oh, and a were-creature. That was not something he could leave the possibility of getting out there.

Especially in these circumstances.

Bohai looked into Li's face and grinned when he saw the flicker of consequences flow through his eyes. He could afford to be cocky now. Once Li let him go, Bohai backed off and moved around the table in the room, keeping the shotgun pointed at Li. "Not to be rude, but I don't like being choked. I was sure that you'd come round to the potential issues for you, though."

Bohai shifted unconsciously. How fast Li moved had shaken him. He'd barely managed to get the sawn-off shotgun out and up in time.

"Now, I have made various arrangements that should aid you. Any attack I can arrange on an ally of the so-called Queen would be welcomed, I am sure." Bohai said, a sober expression on his face. In his head, he added, 'What I have arranged will be even more appreciated. Arranging a situation where we have two enemies hurting each other, even at the possible cost of some of the covert routes to supply these people weapons, will almost certainly give me a promotion.'

Bohai snorted, "I would suggest you don't go after the civilian population, however. The... woman seems to have an *extreme* reaction whenever people do that. But, that is your choice. I wouldn't want her any hotter on my trail than necessary."

Li nodded to Bohai. Internally he sneered.

If there were Holy Objects or technology there, it wouldn't matter what they did. She would be chasing them down relentlessly.

Fortunately, they had a plan for that. Unfortunately, it could only be used once. A one-use teleportation device keyed to his bloodline. And the object he stole would be *his* family's from then on, increasing their prestige within The Sacred Clan. The teleportation device was not similar to any other technology the Clan had uncovered so far.

The two other samples, the one that had been used first, and the one that they had tried to deconstruct so they could replicate it, had given off massive energy bursts when they activated. But the first one had transported everything in it's immediate vicinity to where the devices had been originally found.

That was why his family had moved their ancestral home to where they had discovered the items.

Li considered this plan worth the risk, assuming he could get the Council of Elders to support it.

CHAPTER THIRTEEN

Inside the Faraday Cage, Beast Caves, Russia

Janna was pacing. Boris knew it was because she didn't like the idea of Boris going inside the Faraday cage. The AI, EI, KI (Kurtherian intelligence) or whatever it might be would have him in its power. She was worried that it might be able to do more than simply talk to one of them.

She'd gone so far as to discuss it with TOM and ADAM. Their interim solution had been to supply a device that would transmit a Kurtherian to Russian and a Kurtherian to English dictionary for the computer and have her place it in the Faraday cage overnight before Gyada and Boris went in.

So, she had it done.

However, she still paced with worry. Neither TOM nor ADAM could tell her in any detail the abilities this computer might have. It was, to them, a blank book. A complete unknown.

They had placed the era of the ship to somewhere between three and five thousand years ago. Starships are an expensive proposition, though. Many continued to be used for as long as a millennium after the technology involved in the building was out of date. After all, they still worked, and generally speaking were still safe to use.

At least as safe anything operating in as dangerous a region as space could be.

Shen's examination of the computer, the speeds that it obviously processed at, and the simple fact that it had been used to assist in reconstructing species DNA, all pointed to it being far more powerful than a standard computer of those eras could be expected to be. It was something that had been custom-built by whoever had flown the ship, or perhaps one of the crewmembers.

That left it a Complete Fucking Unknown. Janna had worked in intelligence, she hated dealing with CFUs. Her job had been to make sure that there was nothing out there that was a CFU. And now she was forced to put someone she was fast coming to consider a friend as well as the first true love of her life in a cage with one.

This did not make her a happy camper, to say the least.

She was almost more frustrated with Boris' insistence that he was the right choice to go in. Surely, with her experience as an intelligence asset, she was the more appropriate choice. But nothing could move Boris on his insistence that it was not the case this time.

If it was a full AI, then they needed someone with leadership responsibilities to communicate with it. Although she had some of those responsibilities, as Boris put it, the buck stopped with him.

He was senior to her, and if something did happen, between her, Paul and Danislav there was still a solid leadership cadre available. Throw in Shen and Alecta, and you had a Leadership Council for all aspects of the community that was being built.

Janna especially disliked that he was placing himself as the most expendable. However, she grudgingly stayed in the village well away from the cave when Boris and Gyada were to enter the Faraday cage. She would still be able to watch what was happening by video link, and communicate with Shen any concerns or requests for action. It had been decided that as Janna, Paul and Alecta were the only other known Wechselbalg derived from Gyada's type of nanites, steps needed to be taken to protect them. It was possible that anything that might occur once the cage was opened could affect them as well.

Therefore, it would be best that they are kept at a safe distance.

Gyada was almost eager to enter the Faraday cage. It was as if she missed the contact she had with the intelligence that was contained within. Boris was significantly more cautious. At least with TOM's dictionary having had significant time to transmit and repeat its information, it should be possible to communicate with the intelligence more easily. Although he didn't show it outwardly, it was with some significant trepidation that he entered the Faraday cage.

They entered the Faraday cage, and nothing happened. At least not immediately. Slowly, Boris heard what seemed to be a louder version of the whisper from months before. Then he heard in a singsong tone in his head

<Who is it that I am speaking to?>

He replied, "Boris, representative of Bethany Anne,

Tzarina of my people, Savior of the White from forces bent on its destruction."

<*Please, Boris, now I have a link with you. It is not necessary for you to speak the words. It will slow our communications significantly for you to speak. It also produces an echo for me that reduces clarity.*>

Boris blinked. The fact that it could make requests on something as significant, at least according to ADAM, as asking him to think the words rather than speak them, raised the probability that it was an AI rather than EI or higher. There was still some argument as to whether it be called a KI of greater or lesser ability between TOM and ADAM last time they spoke.

Boris couldn't give a shit. AI and EI were terms better suited to the purpose he was here for today anyway.

Boris said, *We wish to understand the history of how you ended up here. And of who you ended up here with. Also whether you and your companions encountered the nanites on other worlds first or here. What your purpose might have been in modifying humans so they could change into the form of a creature that had long been extinct on this planet.*

There was a sharp intake of breath from Gyada next to him. Her eyes rolled into the back of her head, her body shook with paroxysms, and whimpers of pain escaped her mouth. Boris looked at the box with fear, and anger. If it were going to torture her, to threaten or make an example to him of its power, he would have none of. He rose from the squat he'd been in and slowly moved towards the box hoping that it was unable to do the same thing to him either from the changes to his nanites programming that

TOM had instituted or because it was too focused on Gyada.

Before he reached the box, he heard a hoarse whisper from Gyada, "Stop, Boris. She wanted more... something. Information? Context maybe? She doesn't want to be misunderstood."

Boris paused where he was, but remained standing. He did not move back towards where he had been previously. "Couldn't she have *warned* me? Or asked you? I assume she has a fair idea of how volatile Weres can be. Especially considering she was both present in one form or another when you killed one of her companions and that she was responsible for creating both my ancestors and *you*."

The voice in his head replied in a flat, mechanical, almost crystalline and cutting tone.

<I asked you to think rather than speak. It was necessary for me to find out what had been going on in the time I have lost contact with all outside this rocky enclosed formation.>

Boris twitched at that. He was a little confused. By using over specific terminology, his estimate of her capabilities lowered. He knew Cave had to be in the dictionary provided, but she had gone to precise language. It seemed possible now that she could be simply a very capable EI. That was something he would have to continue doing throughout this conversation. Raising and lowering his estimates of her capabilities. Especially whether she was capable of forming a moral distinction for her actions.

We wish to know the history of your vessel and how it came to its end here.

<Accessing files... Please wait>

Boris sat there, waiting. He glanced at Gyada, she was covered in a thin sheen of sweat. Here and there it collected formed droplets on her face and arms. "Are you okay, Gyada?" He asked in a quiet voice, filled with concern. She nodded.

"She was far more gentle than when the devil asked her to rip information about what the region was like from my mind when he first brought me here." She shuddered in memory. "I was in pain for weeks. I think it was because that creature had wanted the information so fast. I was twitching on the floor for at least a day even after the pain stopped. Later he had told me that he accidentally stripped my neurons. I had no idea what he was trying to say at the time. He used the threat of doing it again to stop me from attacking him when he brought my children here. Once they were out of his power I risked it. Any pain was acceptable to me to prevent him inflicting that on my children."

Both of them twitched when the computer said *<Integrating Subject 143971 Alpha Rho into communications network>* Boris missed Gyada's startled blink at the term. *<Brief summary as follows. Note that exact translation for some specific terms are not possible, and therefore approximations are substituted instead. The ship was stolen five Earth solar centuries after implementation of the 'Shepherd' program. Small groups of dissidents had come to the conclusion that the ultimate manifestation of said program was genetically manipulating galactic races to speed up their development. The conflict was likely in this case between the Shepherded races. Dissidents concluded it was more desirable to speed up genetics alone rather than use unspecified energies on societal modification attempts that would inevitably be wasted.>*

<Stealing a newly retrofitted ship, a group of Twenty-three

Kurtherians embarked on the ship to do what they could to expedite the evolution of species a planet at a time. They were limited to viral genetic insertions at the time they left. Nanite technology was discovered on the 14th planet they visited. By this time eight of the crew were dead, three had remained behind on previous planets to watch races they found interesting for one reason or another. Those three and seven of the remaining crew had mastered the Etheric to the point they no longer required cryogenic capsules during time in between planets or while computer cycles were compiling research.>

There are possibly, what, fifteen odd other from this ship on Earth?

<Negative. After completing a survey of the 29th planet to be explored by the group, there was an unexpected power failure in the Etheric generator. It had been designed for a minimum of three centuries further use under standard power draw. It failed early. Unfortunately for the crew, this happened as the vessel was in flight. While six attempted to channel the Etheric into the Gravitic Drive, the seventh and the original leader, called 'Chaos is in Limited Options,' formed an Etheric field around himself, this unit, the Laboratory, and the maintenance workshop. This was to ensure survival in the case of a catastrophic landing. Such a landing occurred. Five of the six Etheric masters died on impact, the sixth was fatally injured. None of those individuals unable to draw on the Etheric survived the initial failure due to sudden power loss to their Cryogenic pods>

<The Etheric field prevented total destruction of the facilities required to continue the project. Destruction of the ship restricted the project to this planet. Within weeks of landing, advanced nanite technology was discovered to have been inflicted on members of the local population in this region. Reverse engi-

neering it required the sacrifice of these beings, in part due to their aggression.>

The computer continued to give a so-called summary in such detail that Boris dreaded any such detailed form to come. He was lost five minutes further into the computer's brief. Too much new information. *Stop. I need time to go over everything. Do you have something you can transfer the data into that could be read by a...*

<Data transferred into the device with the translation guide. Original and translated versions, as well as complete summary file.>

Thank you

CHAPTER FOURTEEN

Etheric Empire Battleship Archangel.

TOM had rushed a pod down to pick up the new data. Both he and ADAM were curious as to what it contained. Boris had warned them that it was likely to include a history slanted to show the group in a favorable light. At least that was his experience in any report he'd ever seen written. Except for those few reports that had been used against the Nazis at the Nuremberg trial. It was something that just wasn't done.

After uncoupling a couple of EIs from other duties, ADAM put them to work going through the sheer volume of data. There were tens of terabytes of data that had been provided. Only a tiny fraction of that was what TOM and ADAM were looking for to analyze and formulate a report to Boris and Bethany Anne. They needed to know the basics of what had occurred, not the detail of the individual reactions to the experimentation performed.

ADAM considered the information may well be useful later, but it was not something that was in the realm of what Bethany Anne liked or required. The brief summary that the computer at the crash site had provided was completely useless for their purposes.

<<TOM, can you take a look at these names for me? They don't seem to follow the naming conventions of Kurtherians you have previously described to me.>>

'Chaos is in Limited Options,' 'Improvement is Personal, not Societal'... No, none of these follow the naming conventions I previously described to you. They seem to be based on philosophical concepts or beliefs. They also show a general disrespect for the original Shepherd beliefs.

It would seem that, given the timeline provided, there were dissidents well before the history I was taught, which acknowledged the split of the twelve.

What amazes me is that they managed to steal and flee in a newly refurbished ship four and a half thousand years ago. The Shepherd vessels were closely guarded and secured then to prevent amateurs irretrievably corrupting societal matrices. Also, much of the technology they used was archaic by the standards on which my ship was deployed. For example, we stopped commonly using cryogenics only five hundred or so years later, about four thousand years ago. It was utilized for some few purposes. Most people willing to travel or be transported by space were really going on trips too short to require it with current technology or had enough ability with Etheric to make it unnecessary.

<<When should we tell Boris and Bethany Anne that the report will be ready?>>

Tom stopped and thought about it. Even once they cut

out all the experimental data, travel conditions and other extraneous status information that the computer's programming had felt was included in the question, there was still at least half a terabyte of data to wade through. Four and a half thousand years of history could not be compressed to a small size unless you just touched on the high points. A lot of it was quite boring day-to-day matters, but still...

"So, do you guys feel that you have a summary that just hits the high points?" Bethany Anne asked TOM and ADAM as they linked across a conference call. Many people were listening in. To avoid too much confusion, only six had permission to pose questions during the conference call. Bethany Ann, TOM, ADAM, Janna, Boris, and Gyada were the selected few.

"Yes, Bethany Anne," TOM began, "I'll open with a brief summary. It seems that the history of the ship involves a group of dissidents that were around four and a half thousand of your solar years before the present day. They believed strongly that the Shepherd project was doomed to fail. To prove their radical theories, they stole a ship to enact their experiments. Of the original crew of twenty-three, the records confirm all but three are definitively deceased. The last was killed by Gyada eight hundred years ago. The remaining three are not present on Earth, and because the means by which they describe the planets those three chose to stay behind on, I have no definitive location for the remaining three potential survivors."

"So on top of the various Kurtherian factions you already told us about, these twelve clans, we also have three rogue Kurtherians that we know of?" Bethany Anne scowled as she spoke

TOM answered, "To put it simply, yes. It is also interesting to note, that based on their names, there was some disagreement amongst the dissidents as to whether personal or physical perfection was preferable. An interesting side note is that out of the twenty-nine planets they visited, their leader considered Humans to have the most flexible societal make-ups. He had started considering that societal make-up may be a factor in the development of any species. Humans also adapted and invented new technologies at a faster rate than the vast majority of species previously encountered by the dissidents. They were also well behind all other species at the time of contact."

There was a pause before TOM continued, "He put this down to a late evolutionary development of sentients on Earth."

"So we're fast, but late?" she asked.

ADAM interrupted at this point, "That is an imponderable at this time. Twenty-nine data points are not enough to reach a conclusion, and the contact records in TOM's database only adds another ten or twenty. He was not given a full database of past contacts. Only records of particularly successful Shepherd project contacts."

There was silence in the room, then TOM picked up again. "This information is to give a baseline of what this group was working from. They started with viral insertion genetic technology, which was considered well outdated in my time. So much so that their records on how to achieve it far surpass my own. Nanite manipulation is far safer and more stable. A viral genetic manipulation can go rogue on you."

Bethany Anne rolled her eyes, "Stop digressing you two. Please get on with the relevant history of these cockspittles."

TOM continued, "The background is important, but I will continue through as fast as I can. This group was made up of possibly the most intelligent segment of their generation. When they encountered a new technology, they adapted it to their purposes. Often taking less than a year to analyze and recreate said technology. The three that remained behind on various planets did so because they found something fascinating or unique about the inhabitants of those planets. Something that appealed to their personal goals, but not the goals of the group as a whole. More than half of these dissidents did not even achieve the level of mastery of the Etheric that I did, however. Without extensive use of the cryogenic pods, now destroyed, they could not have achieved the breadth of lifespan they did. They died when the power source of the ship failed suddenly."

There was a slight pause as everyone considered the death that came to those around the ship, and what they might have done in that situation. TOM spoke into the quiet, "Their leader was not an experienced engineer, and it took him some time to cobble together the crude Etheric generator that is found in the caves today. Eventually, he started exploring his surroundings, and the team had already developed a neural destabilization weapon that could render most species unconscious or incapacitated. It would also cause some considerable pain."

"Using this device, he collected samples for study. Two of his early collections were werewolves. Being somewhat more experienced at modifying existing technology, and having early examples that the group had already modified to their purposes, he was quickly able to adapt these nanites into the persistent and aggressive form found in Boris, Gyada, and others of that line. From his notes, it seemed to be his hope that the bearers of these nanites would eventually become the dominant subspecies on the planet. He also had plans to adapt non-mammalian forms somehow into the change, although this never occurred. Apparently his group had never considered giving sentients a non-sentient form to change into until he encountered it on Earth. It causes me to wonder how widespread the transformation ability has been imposed on other species. It is possible that Earth was a testing ground for the concept."

"The remaining Kurtherian had resigned himself to building up Earth's technology base. He wanted to ensure a loyal base of 'followers' to work from. That was his goal when he captured Gyada and found her particularly suited to his new nanites. He underestimated the maternal instinct and drive that she possessed, however, which led to his downfall,"

"There are unfortunately at least two significant holes in the data that has been provided. There is no record of an experimental computer in the initial ship's listing, nor is there a history or time period during which one may have been created. This is concerning to me. Given the over completeness of all other records I have come to a disturbing conclusion."

"Only a very select few know Kurtherian organic computers are Kurtherian brain matter. They are often gifted to society by Kurtherians who no longer wish to live. All data contained is therefore purged. It's considered a great crime to allow the personality of someone who wished to be no longer a part of the world to continue to be trapped inside a computer like that. So all possible measures are taken to prevent it. There is some evidence that when there was a personality to be stuck in a computer after formerly having a body, it would go insane rather quickly."

"The fact that this information is completely missing from the records has led me to the conclusion that there is a Kurtherian personality in the computer. It's not an AI, EI or KI. It's a pre-existing personality running the quantum computer. That makes it anathema."

Gyada was quickly parsing this information as TOM spoke "NO! Over my dead body will you suggest we harm her! She was wise, kind and patient with me while I was trapped in that cave, you ghost! After all, why is it we never see you? Could I come to the conclusion that you are a similar being? I've never seen your physical form."

There was an uncomfortable silence for just a moment before Bethany Anne spoke, "Great, ok, apparently we need to discuss this in a smaller group. Thank you all for listening in." Bethany Anne said as she restricted the conference link solely to the six people critical to the situation.

Bethany Anne went quiet for a moment as she held this conversation mentally.

TOM, Why didn't you at least warn me that you are going to bring this up? I could have told you it would be a bad idea.

Bethany Anne, the situations with me being inside you and this computer are *not* similar. I still have a physical form. I simply happen to be sharing it with you. Although incredibly difficult, I can be extracted into another physical body. If I'm right, this personality is stuck in a box after having lived in a body. Completely different situation. I also admitted at the time that what I did was wrong and it was an accident. There was mild reproach in his tone as he spoke

That's just semantics TOM. One of the greatest strengths of the group we've created is our tolerance for differences. What you said could start breaking that down. I needed to stomp on that immediately.

Bethany Anne, if that is what it is, then it IS an anathema! It can't be allowed to continue for the sake of itself.

Your predeterminations are showing TOM.

There was a muted but charged question from ADAM. <<Is this how you see me TOM? As some form of abomination because I'm in a 'box', not a body?>>

No ADAM. Of course not. You were never in a body in the first place. He was almost dismissive of ADAM's concern.

TOM, is this simply a societal belief, or is there any evidence to back it up?

There was a telling silence from Tom when she asked

this question. He was clearly considering his answer care-fully. **It simply wasn't done in my lifetime. The records clearly stated that bad things happened when it was attempted.**

Do you know when that was? Also, consider they may have found a different method to achieve the same effect. One without those consequences.

TOM was silent again, considering. The stories had been so bad that it was ingrained as a terrible idea within his people. He'd reacted with that knowledge. Reluctantly he answered **No, we are taught fairly consistently that it is** *always* **bad. I hadn't considered alternative techniques with different outcomes. I should have. The Entarians do it occasionally.**

Gyada was fuming silently with Boris raising a hand to her every time she went to speak into the silence. Janna whispered in her ear "Bethany Anne won't put up with that sort of intolerant-sounding behavior. Let her talk it out with TOM."

Finally, Bethany Anne spoke up "TOM and I been discussing his Gott Verdammt surprise revelation. Appar-ently, it is based on some bad experiences the Kurtherians had in their past. It seems to have become something of a taboo subject and action. As we have no idea exactly how her personality was kept intact inside the computer, we'll take it one step at a time. We need to find out why she selectively redacted that information."

"It makes it certain that she is a true intelligence of one form or another, though," ADAM said over the link thoughtfully. "To selectively redact information like that is something that an EI would not consider. It may be the sheer volume of data she supplied was a countermeasure to hide the redaction too. If we didn't have EIs to assist, it would have taken even me a week to fully sort out the data. Especially with everything else I'm doing."

Gyada said, unequivocally, "She's not bad. She wouldn't intentionally cause harm unless ordered to. The only reason she caused me pain when I was in there was that she desperately felt a need for context." Boris glanced at her.

Evidently, she had been hiding some things, but it was more out of concern for what might happen to a friend than anything else. That was something he could respect.

You needed to protect your friends and family in this world.

Bethany Anne let loose a deep sigh, "Well, Boris, you need to go back in and find out why she hid this from us. It is still possible, no offense intended Gyada, that she might mean harm to us. Be careful. But find out her personal history."

CHAPTER FIFTEEN

Moscow, Russia

Ivan had become nervous when he had spotted the former Sergeant Brogonovich in Moscow trailing a Chinese fellow. He decided to keep spying for Janna despite her change of allegiances from the Russian government to this new group that was building the town, New Romanovka up near Archangelsk. He knew exactly how to follow Brogonovich. The man was arrogant in the extreme, with an overconfidence in his abilities to detect a tail.

Ivan believed that Brogonovich had turned traitor. He thought that with Brogonovich's overconfidence and propensity for cruelty, he would surely have been amongst the NVG casualties, and perhaps an unidentified corpse in the pile of bodies that they buried after the attack.

To say Ivan had been surprised to spot him was an understatement.

When Brogonovich managed to get the attention of the Chinese man, Ivan had moved closer. He was willing to take the risk that his former comrade might recognize him in exchange for a possible windfall of information. The two moved into a bar, and Ivan followed them in to try and overhear the conversation, pulling his collar up against his face for concealment.

"... I know you plan on going after the bastard who wiped out most of the NVG. I've managed to gather a fair number of my comrades who escaped the destruction. We would be happy to support you in any attack on his new location." There was a disturbing fire in both Brogonovich's eyes and voice at this. He lowered his voice slightly "I know what you are. Konrad had me slated to be changed into your kind, but then the attacks started happening."

The Chinese man's eyes narrowed at this comment. Ivan felt rather than saw the man shrug it off. Ivan only had the vaguest idea of what they were talking about. "Gather your men in two months at this point." He slid a card across to the treacherous Sergeant. "I will inspect them and see if they will be of value to my forces. There is no need to expend them for little purpose."

Brogonovich's eyes narrowed at that comment, but he gave the small Chinese man a curt nod. "Two months from today we shall be there." He ordered two shots of vodka and slid one to his newfound comrade. It was with carefully hidden distaste that the Chinese man drank down the offered shot. Still, he knew enough about Russians to know that it would have been a grave insult to refuse it.

One that could have possibly *killed* the agreement.

Ivan waited until they had been gone for more than an hour before he left the bar. He had the information he wanted that there is an attack coming against New

Romanovka. There had been no need to risk extra exposure and the loss of that information in tailing one or the other of them further. But why on earth did the Chinese have an interest in New Romanovka?

Wrangling Information, Faraday Cage, New Romanovka, Russia.

This time it was Boris that was nervous about entering the Faraday cage. The revelations from TOM had him concerned. After all, who wants to be trapped in a cage with something that can possibly harm them, and could be completely insane?

This was the situation that Boris faced.

To his surprise, Janna was less concerned. She had spent a significant amount of time talking to Gyada. In that time, Gyada had convinced her of the friendliness of whatever personality the machine contained. In some ways, she was potentially a better source of information on the computer's intelligence than TOM. She had spent eight centuries communicating with it, after all.

So they moved into the cage the next day, with the same setup as previously on Boris' insistence. In Janna's mind that alone showed his nerves. That Boris still felt the need for such extreme precautions showed that he was still greatly concerned with the potential threat that the machine posed. Boris had also decided to attack the problem in a confrontational method. He felt that was the best way through the bullshit and reach a quick solution to the problem.

After he and Gyada had entered the Faraday cage, he

took some time to sit down and center himself. Gyada was nervous for other reasons. Boris had effectively become a provisional judge for her friend. On top of that, he was in her opinion the most likely of the people judging the computer to be sympathetic to its plight.

She kept all of this to herself. Many months ago she hadn't truly understood what a computer was. In theory, Gyada understood, but it was hard for someone from the Iron Age to comprehend their appearance or how they functioned. She felt from how people acted around computers that continuing to declare it 'her friend' would result in her opinion as being less valued. It may even convince them she was at least a little crazy. People seemed to consider computers tools, with no aspect of personage about them.

Boris started his conversational gambit with *I request more information from you. Could you please start with your name?*

The machine responded in its cold crystalline voice with <Error. This device has no such designation. Please clarify.>

Between my allies and I, we have come to the conclusion that you are an intelligence. We have yet to classify what kind of intelligence you might be. There is some argument as to whether you are dangerous or safe. Sane or crazy. But you left a critical gap in the information provided that led to the unanimous conclusion that you're hiding something from us. Hiding exactly what you are. If you wish to receive any form of goodwill, I suggest you stop hiding it from us further.

There was silence for some time after that, at least on Boris' end of the conversation.

The mystery personality was gibbering to Gyada. *<He's bluffing, right? Please tell me he's bluffing! They have a Kurtherian associated with them! They'll consider me an abomination. I'm ... I'm a mixture. The personality survived being transferred from the body into the box. I was dying because of my lover's anger, and he took insane risks to save a part of me.>* There was a pause *<I WANT TO KEEP EXISTING>* and something like a sob could be heard in Gyada's mind.

Gyada responded as calmly as she could, *If there is a Kurtherian, I only heard him talk, I've never seen his body. I called him out on that in the discussion when he insisted that you needed to be destroyed immediately if you had a pre-transferral personality still in existence. The leader, the one he follows, backed me not him. She insisted that we assess you. I think she wants to evaluate you as well. I've never met her in person, although I have seen her.*

<But what do I do? How can he trust me now he knows I've hidden parts of myself from him?>

Boris will understand that Gyada answered as reassuringly as she could. *he's hidden aspects of himself from many people over the years. It's not like people who can change like we can are universally acknowledged as more than a myth by most people according to what I've learned so far. The population of this town is unusual in that the majority know about us. You need to tell Boris the truth. Everything. Even what you haven't told me.*

<I can't. It's not even that I don't want to. It's that I literally can't. The leader placed programming in me that prevents me from detailing it.>

Well, at least tell him that. Maybe there is a solution that can be found.

<I don't want people rummaging around in me - that would be - I don't think I can describe it.> Her communication sounded frayed.

Even to remove that program? And others that might be affecting you in a similar way?

<A Kurtherian could order the block removed. I'm not allowed to tell Kurtherians. The programming, it hurts me when I get close to telling anyone...> There was hesitation and a strange static feeling in Gyada's head before the computer continued, with something missing from what she had apparently planned to say. *<Most Kurtherians would order me to wipe myself. They would see it as a kindness, not as ordering me to suicide. What do I do, child? Who do I trust?>*

Gyada was shocked by her friend's reaction. In all the time she had spent with the computer, Gyada had never thought to ask it for a name. Gyada had found it calm, willing to be her mental companion and always authoritative when teaching her something. Now it wasn't only acting panicked, it was asking her for a solution to its problems.

With all the aid and company she'd been given over the years, she had to think carefully. What would be the best way for it to explain the situation? She understood where Boris stood on this issue. If the computer really were a danger to anyone under his protection, then it would have to be destroyed.

She knew it wasn't his preferred option, but he was a leader. He knew his responsibilities. He would carry through on it if it were necessary. It saddened her, but because he wasn't leaping to conclusions it didn't particularly upset her.

Finally, she thought she'd come up with an answer. *You don't really want to speak to Boris until you can give him the whole truth do you?*

There was some hesitation before Gyada received a reply. <*No, I don't. I've already fostered enough distrust between him and I. I also don't want any Kurtherian anywhere near me or in contact with me. Your Kurtherian might not even mean to do it, but if he's afraid enough of what I might be, that could be enough for him to make me wipe myself from existence.*>

<*The leader never told me what the exact programming was. Chaos is in Limited Options simply laughed and said he was probably the only one who would lift it.*>

I may have a solution. There is an AI that seems to work closely with the Kurtherian. I suspect he is, after Boris, most likely be sympathetic to you due to the similarities in your natures. At worst he is your best chance of getting the programming removed one way or the other. He is concerned that you might try to modify him. That is why there are all these elaborate physical firewalls between his contacts with you.

<*But how will you convince him that I mean him no harm? I wouldn't hurt another electronic identity. That would be... Like a Kurtherian deliberately stabbing other Kurtherians, we just can't harm each other, not with the trauma after the wars. We changed our race, steadily reducing our capacity for violence. Violence against other races was hard enough. Only a few of my group could use the neural destabilization device in self-defense against other species. It's just not in us to be aggressive toward other species.*>

Something about all that was decidedly odd to Gyada. After all, it was now clear to her that the core of the computer in this box was a Kurtherian brain. Did that mean that some form of violence had to have been committed against the body that had previously held it?

Or was the computer hinting at the complete insanity of her previous leader?

Gyada knew until a solution was found, there was no way of finding the answers to these questions. Without these answers, Boris and Bethany Anne would be forced to destroy her.

Rising from her chair she indicated the exit with her hands to Boris. They had things they had to do before they could complete this task. She felt Boris would understand why the computer had chosen to reveal these things to her rather than both of them. But they needed to be able to talk it over with ADAM as well.

CHAPTER SIXTEEN

Various places, Conference Call.

"I spent hours trying to work with the system. Every time I access it as a Kurtherian might I got this message. I do not understand what it means. Some code perhaps? I can't figure out what the key might be." ADAM told the group. "That restricts my attempts to break whatever programming might be limiting her through that means. She has asked us to 'review the message and find the answer.'"

There was a pause before he continued, "My communications with her was suddenly severed once she said that. Gyada assured me that she is still there. Gyada can still feel the 'murmuring' as she describes it." Gyada nodded at that, and ADAM continued, "I suspect the program warns when she gets close to triggering some sort of threshold that would delete her. Or it could be caused by some sort of 'self-preservation' program. Also, she continues to insist she has no name."

There was a pause before Bethany Anne spoke, "I'm not getting any younger here, ADAM. Spit it out."

"Of course. The best translation I believe is this. 'Found before I'm proven, absent once realized. I am seen most clearly in utter darkness, never to be found in the light. To be found commonly in battle, rarely near the hearth. The Poor find me easily, but the Rich find me easy to lose. What am I?'" He transmitted the original Kurtherian to TOM. "Do you agree TOM?"

TOM's voice came over the communication line, "There are a few words that are possibly confused in it. But their meaning could have shifted slightly over the three and a half thousand years between when they left and when I left. I imagine it is as close as we are going to get." Tom agreed, "In some ways, it's very clever. Kurtherians as a whole aren't particularly good at riddles. Codes, science, math, yes. Riddles? Not really our thing. Definitely not mine or something my clan focused on. Whoever made this wasn't your average Kurtherian."

"And neither are you, TOM, you're just not average in a different way. Damn." Bethany Anne said. "Give me someone to shoot or chop into tiny pieces, and I'm fine. Riddles are not the sort of thing I'm good at. I can piece together hard facts to form a picture, but this is some sort of Gottverdamm abstract, I think. Why did the spelunking asshole diver have to be into riddles of all things? Boris, sorry, your computer, your riddle at this point. Work with your team and get us involved as needed. I've got a stupid meeting with those on Earth again. Talk soon."

There was a click as she disconnected from the call,

leaving the group to discuss the riddle on their own. Janna commented "I wish she'd left TOM on the line. I have no idea how Kurtherians think, and that could be key to solving the riddle. Damn it. How anachronistic is it that the quickest way to solve our problem is to answer a riddle."

"Enough," Boris said, glaring at her. "I doubt TOM would be as much help as you think. From what has been discussed he seems to be a more 'conventional' Kurtherian than the one who wrote the riddle. He even admitted that the language may have resulted in slight meaning shifts. I suppose when you live as long as they seem to that language shifts more slowly." He grimaced at that, going over his memory of how different Russian was from the language of his youth. "We have been given a job by our Czarina. We will do that job. Come, give me some suggestions."

There was silence. Shen had a focused expression on his face, then he reached for a pen and paper and started breaking down the riddle into four pieces, putting potential answers to each of the paired statements. Once he was finished, he passed it around. Janna took it first. Out of the Russians, her English was, in some ways oddly, the best. After all, Danislav was three or four times her age and Boris was far older.

As they handed it to the group, Paul glanced at Gyada, and with a twitch of his head caught her attention. "While they work on that part of it, we need to work on the other part. Do you have a feel for what the author of the Riddle might have been like? Has the unnamed personality given you any idea? More to the point do you have any idea? Out of everyone here, it's just you two that could give us some idea of what he was like."

Gyada looked at him then narrowed her eyes "I believe the English term from how I saw him is 'Bat-shit crazy'. Completely nuts was my perception. Always talking to himself or the air around him. What difference does that make?" Gyada shifted uncomfortably.

Paul was very strange to her in many ways. In her time, she would have considered him a follower of Loki. A capable fighter, and from everything she had heard, not without courage. He always seemed to have a jest available and didn't appear to see combat as anything more than a job. Something that he had to do, not something that was filled with honor and glory. He trained his militia to approach war in the same fashion. War, to him, was simply business. It was more of a profession like smithing or farming than the calling she remembered it being for her.

Paul cleared his throat. "Can you be a little more specific? And could he have been talking to the computer, not himself?" Gyada paused in thought. Could he have been? It wasn't like she understood the language he spoke at the time. She thought back to that time very carefully.

Going over her memories, which were surprisingly clear.

The memory jumped on her and left her frozen. The strange looking creature. How it acted, constantly muttering and tinkering with devices in that cave that seemed to disappear. She had tried to find it when she first became trapped, but the cave walls were all solid. The thing that stood out most was the constant muttering.

Then the hidden ... she shuddered and shied away from that memory.

She shook herself lightly, then answered, "Going back into those memories isn't fun you know. Sometimes the strange being might have been talking to her. Sometimes it was definitely a mutter to himself. And I don't know what he was saying, I didn't know the language at that time."

"Fair enough. Okay, that means he had some narcissistic tendencies in human terms. Probably a bit of a jerk to anyone around him, especially women of his own race." Paul muttered to himself, focused on what he was hearing. Janna had been listening into the conversation and her eyes went wide as Paul started trying to psychoanalyze the alien. First, because, well how did one psychoanalyze a totally different race and species? Secondly, because he always played the fool. The buffoon, the idiot, the jokester.

Even when training townspeople in their militia duties he did it with jokes and funny situations gotten in and out of.

Always to emphasize the skills he was teaching.

This was a completely different Paul, one who was deadly serious. One who wasn't playing the idiot. Janna assumed he'd been there outside of combat, but this was the first time she'd noticed him do this in front of her.

"What do you mean by all that? Besides, where did you get any training to be able to assess someone's psychological state?" Janna asked sharply. Paul had taken training the townspeople into a militia onto his own shoulders. It left him little time for much else, and he was always acting the clown in the meetings of the heads of departments. He was always around, but not where she was.

Paul blushed and looked away. Alecta rolled her eyes and answered. "He has two different masters degrees in psychology. One in aberrant psychology, the other in Combat and Post-Combat psychology. It's why I get so frustrated when he acts the fool. He's at least as smart as me, and he insists on playing his version of Prince Myshkin."

Paul went back to looking at Gyada. "Is there anything else about the alien that seemed strange? Compare how he acted to how the personality acts."

Gyada said, "No, I've said enough. I don't need to keep going about how he was." Her face was pale and her voice shook as she whispered, "It's too painful."

"And being effectively enslaved to a person, possibly the person who tried to kill you, wouldn't be?" Paul asked quietly, caring. "She can't even tell us if that's what happened. I'm not sure, but it is possible. I just need a few more details. I can't tell you what I'm looking for - it could taint what you remember. Please... It could be key to answering the Riddle. A riddle's answer is as much an arti-fact of the person who created it as anything." There was pleading in his voice.

He looked up at the others "Keep going. I'm only working on something that will help us narrow down the answers you guys come up with."

Shen meanwhile was going another route. He still had a way to communicate with ADAM from his laptop. He quickly typed a message 'See what you can do about getting an analysis of this Kurtherian group's leaders actions - I think his name is Chaos is in Limited Options.

See if you can get any information relevant to his state of mind to someone for a quick psychological analysis.'

The response came back 'Timeframe longer than BA will be happy with. Two to three weeks minimum.'

Shen muttered "Fuck, I hate reality. Working with computers is so much easier." There went his second idea. He had no real idea on what to do next. He looked around the room. Gyada wasn't going to be that much help with the notes. She simply hadn't known English that long. Hell, Shen was surprised with the fact they hadn't asked for a Russian translation. He went to rise, but Boris waved him back down. With nothing immediate to do, he relaxed enough that an idle thought occurred to him... one he didn't like much. He liked his life alone, working the black market and various scams.

He didn't like representing his father's business that much, but that was what allowed him to travel, gave him the other opportunities.

He was slowly becoming a valuable member of Boris' inner circle. Worse, he found himself appreciating the feelings of trust, safety, and respect that created in him. *Damn*, he thought, *does that make me a sucker for my saviors or a sucker for a cause? At least one that has most of the facts that I know worked into it?*

He was left with that thought, a slightly forlorn look on his face.

Boris now had the pad and was going over everything carefully. He had a soft smile on his face. He was hopeless at riddles but enjoyed them anyway. Of course, the fact that he was working in English, which he had only learned in the last century or so, complicated the matter for him.

He was always thinking in Russian, then translating back and forth. He only added a word or two to each of the four sections. He passed the pad on to Alecta and turned his focus on Paul.

It wasn't often Paul acted seriously. He was always thoughtful in combat, but Boris had seen him avoid a mugging by laughing in the face of the guy who pulled a knife. He was a little unnerving in the way he could get out of any situation he got into.

The closest Paul had come to dying had been in situations where Boris had asked for his help. When counter-sniping in Afghanistan he'd used a really odd trick. He had put a small mirror on a wire that gave away a false position to the enemy. It seemed stupid to most people, but Boris agreed that if it's stupid and works, it ain't stupid.

"Okay, so he tried to act cold and dispassionate, but you felt that he was enjoying the pain that he caused?" Paul asked Gyada,

"Yes. If I felt he might be as sadistic as the first man to approach my Father for permission to court me. If he hadn't been I might have risked not taking the actions I did. But there was a sense of excitement about the pain he caused. The cruelty was as much an end in itself as a means to an end."

"Hum. I think I have enough to help narrow down the list."

He turned to Boris and the others. "Have you finished that list and narrowed down by removing answers that fit only one?" They gathered round the table, eliminating answers that only covered one or two pieces of the puzzle.

Finally, they were left with a half dozen: Fire, Despair, Fear, Nothing, Hope, and Grace.

"Well, Fire is definitely out," Gyada commented. "Most hearths have a fire after all."

"I'd drop Grace and Nothing. Grace doesn't fit being easily found in battle, and that pair doesn't make sense with Nothing as the answer to them at all."

There was silence. They had narrowed it down to three. "Fear doesn't fit as well with the first pair of clues either," Alecta suggested. "Hope and Despair both seem to answer it, though. Maybe Hope is a better fit, but Despair still works." Janna narrowed her eyes, then nodded slowly in agreement.

All eyes turned to Paul. "It's so nice to be appreciated for my mind," He said with a lopsided grin.

Alecta whacked him on the back of the head. "It'd happen far more often if you'd stop acting like a clown," she grumbled.

Paul shrugged while rubbing the back of his head. That was true enough after all. "Now, which one would a narcissistic sadist use? It comes down to blocking off her ability to tell anyone the answer. However, he managed that. If he'd left her able to tell anyone the answer would be Despair. Plus, he'd have made it harder for her to communicate at all. Because he made her unable to give the answer, but only put otherwise light restrictions on her ability to communicate, I'd bet on *Hope*. Hard to be certain if he'd lost touch with reality completely but Hope is the more likely answer all things considered. It would have been another way for him to torture the personality."

· · ·

Suddenly, all hell broke loose on the systems. Alarms blared in the conference room.

"I swear, it wasn't me." Paul smiled.

Boris typed in a code to the computer in the room and said, "No, it wasn't." He turned the screen to face the others.

One of the twenty-four assets or someone from their families had triggered their panic button.

CHAPTER SEVENTEEN

Moscow, Russia

Ivan and Anton had been tasked to keep an eye on the Chinese after Ivan submitted his report to Janna. They were to set up a signal intelligence intercept on the Chinese intelligence outpost in Moscow. They knew the frequencies that the Russian bugs would be using. This enabled them to catch anything for those devices. They also set up listening posts on several of the windows. These would burst transmit any recordings back to their daytime operations site.

All in all, it was a tidy, if undermanned, operation. If they weren't getting support from New Romanovka on the analysis side, there wouldn't be much point to it. But they were, and most of their duties involved making sure the systems were still running.

After two weeks, orders came down to track down and capture the agent called Bohai from the outpost. He seemed to be taking too much interest in New Romanovka for Boris to be happy with. Taking him out was a risk, as it might make the Chinese more curious. But if he were taken by Russians, it might also look like an official government operation, which could dissuade the Chinese from continuing to investigate the town. They had enough problems without aggravating the Russian government.

Denying that someone got pissed off enough at you to flatten a mountain tended to leave you with a lot of internal problems. Denying to the outside world that it happened, when there were plenty of satellites that could see the evidence was really quite silly.

Ivan and Anton also knew there were a half-dozen personages that they might be requested to extract. Therefore, it was only a mild surprise when they got a request to call in over the specialized equipment.

"Sleepy to Mama Bear. Requested contact initiated."

"Enemy activity around Laborer. Beacon sent. Request you remove Laborer's family to outskirts of Hive. Pack will be in support. Pickup will meet you in no more than four hours."

Despite the supposed security of the special communications network, Janna insisted on using code names and operational terms. Evgenni had triggered his *get me out* beacon. Someone would be sent in a pod to pick him up. Ivan and Anton were to get his family out of harm's way in case they became secondary targets. They should have up to four additional assets en route and should move towards the outskirts on foot until their supports arrived.

Ivan was pissed off now. It was probably those Chinese fuckers that were involved. Why his own government hadn't cleared them out, he'd never know.

The philosophy that it was better to know who the

enemy spies were and where they were only made sense up to a point. The fact that this outpost was the only one that the Russians closely watched made it certain that there were other sites the Chinese had, that the government had never found out about.

"We know you talked to Boris, Evgenni. Helped him cut a deal with the government so they wouldn't harass him further. That would be enough for us to take you and torture you. That you might have additional information that could be useful to us?" He looked over at the man, "is just the icing on the cake."

Bohai said this as he took a needle to a medical vial of fluid. "I can never remember what this stuff is called. I don't really need to know. All I need to know is it will increase the amount of pain you feel by a factor of ten at a minimum. That is for people who are particularly insensitive to its effects."

Evgenni's heartbeat had increased significantly when the needle came out. He didn't like needles, and the thought of what might be in the needle disturbed him further. However, he'd also been responsible for checking the structural integrity of many buildings in NVG sites. Nothing in this room matched the carnage potential he'd seen fulfilled at those sites. Arms ripped off, some fast, some slow. Bodies completely eviscerated, with blood trails indicating that despite a significant percentage of their organs being on the ground, the person involved had still been alive for some time.

He knew what Boris and his people were capable of. He doubted the Chinese had the same... Potential. He was clinging to the hope that he had managed to get off the signal to Boris for his people. He had been briefed on Boris' history, and he knew that if it was Boris who turned up, the five Chinese spies in the room and outside its door would be slabs of meat before the night was over.

Whether he was alive at that time or not.

"Somehow Gyada got wind of this mission Boris. She is insisting she is ready to go. She's promised not to change and has already collected several axes and knives," Danislav was telling his father figure with some trepidation.

After weeks of training with the woman from the past, he just outright feared her. "She's even promised to follow my lead. Not that I'm sure she will, but she might. She's realized that there are a lot of different dangers in the world today, from what they were in her time."

Boris glared at his second in command, "How the hell did she find out about the mission?" He growled.

"She claims she could smell the excitement from the caves. Besides, we have been talking about doing training missions for several weeks now. Ever since Bethany Anne dropped a handful of mark two pods on us, for our use. You said she'd be cleared for those training runs. She seems to assume that means she's authorized for this, too."

Boris grunted.

They'd been keeping her clear of the major cities, although some of the Weres had taken her with them to a couple of the larger towns in the oblast. "This is something you have to answer honestly then, Danislav. Do you see her as a potential asset or detriment to the mission profile?"

He quickly opened his mouth to answer, then paused. He thought about her skill with ax, knife and in hand-to-hand. If they wanted to keep this mission below the radar, which they did, she would definitely be an asset.

She might behave oddly on the streets, but most Russians would take that to mean she was drugged or drunk. It wasn't particularly uncommon to see intoxicated people in the area where the beacon was now transmitting.

And if all hell broke loose and the op was blown she'd shift, which would give them an edge in getting away. It was against orders but...

In team training, she'd shown a vicious maternal instinct to those on her side. To the point where Paul had to caution her and suspend her from training for a week. But that could be an advantage in this situation. Danislav knew she'd be focused on protecting the mission's primary, to an extent no one else he'd met could.

"Given the mission, I have to say that she would be a significant asset and a slight liability. At least we know she doesn't freeze with gunfire if it comes to that. And to be honest, I've only encountered maybe two dozen who are better naturally at close combat fighting than she. Finally, it prevents me from asking if Janna or Paul are available. We don't know if this is the Chinese government or the Sacred Clan after all. Both groups would have a hard on to take out anything we consider an asset after what Bethany Anne did."

Boris grunted in agreement at that. Then he sighed and

answered, "Fine, she goes. But warn her that if she operates outside the limits that we defined that it will be the last time I let her go on an operation. Nothing further than close patrols for three months minimum if she screws this one up."

The rescue squad's final composition was three Spartans, four Weres, Danislav, and Gyada. It might have seemed overkill, but the Chinese had co-opted one of the local gangs. For all Janna knew, they were walking into a crossfire ambush.

The Weres spread out, covering potential exit points between them and surveying the bystanders. It was nighttime in a warehouse district. There was only a small group of gang members two buildings across.

The Spartans brought their carbines up from under their coats to their shoulders. Danislav set to preparing a breaching charge for the door. Gyada gave him a quizzical look, then moved back 10 paces and shoulder charged the door. It flew inwards with a 'crack-thump' and a shriek of tortured metal. While it was noisy, it was still quieter than the breaching charge would have been.

Danislav and the Spartans were simply surprised that anyone as relatively small as her could take out a steel door.

Danislav was even more impressed that she wasn't worried about potential injuries from such an action. He could have done it, but his shoulder would have been bruised for the next half hour. He was also a good 20 kg larger than her in human form. That's why he brought along the breaching charge from the pod once they downloaded building schematics and details.

They also had to rush to catch up to the disappearing woman. The moments that they'd stood there stunned by her actions hadn't slowed her down a bit. There was the glint of an ax in one of her hands. Then the distinctive sound of a silenced gunshot.

They caught up just in time to see her hit the shooter with the first swing across the chest, back swing across the throat and a third swing to the groin, where she embedded the ax.

He went down with a quiet gurgle. There wasn't much chance that he'd last long. She paused only to remove her second ax from her belt. Danislav stopped long enough to remove the one embedded in the poor bastard and sped him on his way.

Gyada pushed through, past her falling victim, as if she was following something. All Danislav could smell was the blood and evacuated bowels from her most recent victim. Before that, all he'd been able to smell was the rubbish and detritus from the poorly maintained district.

Something had caught her attention, though. He thought it had to be a scent. She certainly couldn't have seen anything. Nor could he hear anything, so he doubted it was something she heard.

Danislav managed to catch up with her before they entered the next room, cursing her and telling her to slow down. They were leaving the Spartans well behind them. That meant they were losing any cover fire, and probably that three pissed off Spartans were trailing them.

Danislav had never met a single special forces trooper who liked missing a fight.

Gyada charged for the door that was guarded by a half dozen thugs. They were barely better trained than the average peasant from her time. Brawlers, perhaps, but no real skill behind them. One of them, a beefy Slavic man, interposed himself between her and the door. All that did was give her some cushioning as she slammed him into the door and knocked it down.

Danislav grunted as he saw two of the thugs follow her through the doorway. The other three turned to face him. One had a length of chain, the other two drew pistols. Ducking a swing of the chain Danislav focused on the nastier threat. *This is why you set a pace that your fire support could match, damn it*, ran through his mind. He managed to swing the ax into the hand drawing a pistol before it could fire. Following it up with a punch to the solar plexus, he put that target out of the fight for some time.

The chain whipped across his back as he turned. A second quick blow wrapped the chain around his upper thigh, and he felt a tug. A grin crossed his face. This was a really bad break of luck.

For his attacker.

There was not enough leverage to pull him down. Maybe if the blow had caught his ankle, but with it wrapped around his upper thigh that attacker was now at Danislav's mercy. Which was another way of saying *no mercy*.

He spun in place and switched the ax to his left hand. Grabbing the chain, he yanked the man forward and cleaved his skull in two. The vicious blow cost him his weapon, though. Disarmed, he saw the final thug bring a pistol into line. He raised the body of the dead man in front of him, hoping he'd moved fast enough. Six shots rang out, compressed into too short a time to come from one gun.

His ears ringing from the gunfire, he slowly lowered the body. Once his vision was clear of the corpse he saw the three Spartans clear the room. Evidently, they'd all shot both thugs... once.

Moving through the blood-spattered room, one of them said, "Chief, it's best to stay with the team."

"Tell Gyada that when you catch her, will you?" Danislav bitched. They filed past him as he unwrapped himself.

The Spartan blanched. With how she had broken through the doors, together with the speed at which she moved, he wasn't sure he wanted to say anything that might upset her.

Especially considering how brutally she'd taken out the first thug.

"Clear!" came back a quick report and Danislav stopped trying to rush himself.

When the Spartans came back into the room a little while later, it was with a blood-covered and somewhat cut up Evgenni. "Boss, you're going to need to talk to her. Severe Post Combat reaction... I think."

There was a decidedly odd expression on the Spartan's face. "We'll get him to the pod. If we need to, we'll send for another one, but he's not too bad. Just need to keep him outta shock."

They moved past him towards the exit and the pod.

There might have been some growls and snarls outside, but a sudden keening focused Danislav's attention on Gyada. It was with some trepidation he entered the room.

There were four bodies in the chamber. Three looked like relatively normal kills for this kind of fight, complete with an ax sticking out of what looked to be the torturer's chest. There was a scalpel in that man's hand at least. The fourth looked like some beast had ripped it apart.

Gyada was rocking in a corner, one of her arms held close to her chest. It was covered in blood and looked strange. That was because it wasn't a human arm. For some reason, and the Gods knew how, she'd shifted just that arm into her beast form's arm.

With care, concern and a calm voice, he managed to get her moving back to the pod. What the other's reaction would be, he had no idea.

CHAPTER EIGHTEEN

Computer Central, Beast Caves, Archangel Oblast, Russia

Danislav had Evgenni sent to the infirmary, then set about searching the base for Boris. Paul had met the pod upon finding out about Gyada's condition. His face was blanched, and as he passed Danislav, he said, "You and Boris didn't ask my opinion on her inclusion on this jaunt why?"

Medics rushed past them to take Evgenni to the infirmary.

Danislav blinked, "It was an operational matter. Was she capable of being an asset or not was what we considered."

Paul's lips pressed together as he hissed, "You brainless numbskulls! She was tortured! She still has obvious trauma from that, and you sent her into a situation where the goal was to rescue someone being tortured? How bloody stupid was it?"

There was a grim turn to Paul's voice, one that Danislav had never heard, "I know it was bad, Spec-ops take a bit to be… impressed. But *how* horrible on a scale of one to ten, with five being what you'd expect from an operation with no enemy survivors?"

Danislav had to think about it for a little while. He wanted to equivocate, tell Paul it hadn't been that bad. His scale, however, meant that the mission rated a minimum of five. You don't get the hostage back on a rescue mission without a certain level of carnage. And if you lied to Paul, and anyone found out, Boris would find out and be angry at you. He definitely didn't want what was behind door number two.

"Somewhere between eight and a half and a nine. She ripped out one of the bastards' rib cage. Hell, she still hasn't managed to change back from her partial change. We can do that? No one ever told me that." Paul nodded at the first part, then looked up with a scathing glance at the attempted distraction.

"They think it's related to the ability to transform into a Pricolici. I haven't tried, and I wouldn't want to. This is the first time I've heard of anyone who can't take the hybrid form being able to make a partial change. They don't tell me everything. You'd better find Boris and give him a report. He already knows I consider you and him far more at fault for anything Gyada might have suffered on the op. Now I just need to find out if this might have helped her, or ruined any chance of recovery." Paul walked back over to where he had Alecta taking Gyada back to her room.

Danislav found Boris in what was becoming known as the computer room. A feminine voice was saying "Without the appropriate historical-religious background I cannot give myself a name. My former one is no longer appropriate. Now, with the chains of CILO's programming released, I can choose a name, but will not take one that does not fit the context of this planet."

Shen quipped at her "admit it, at least part of the reason you're asking this is that you've been bored faster. Besides, we haven't assessed where you're staying. How can we trust that giving you all the information won't send you loopy? Or loopier?"

"Sanity is not something that you will find fits any being unless the meaning is re-crafted to suit their particular psyche." The computer stated primly. Then somewhat disturbingly, it giggled. "You worry too much about my sanity. If I operate outside your desired limitations, you can always trap me back in the Faraday cage simply by turning it back on. This unit has not been maintained for eight centuries, and even with nanites repairing the casing it would take years to properly fix. The only other unit theoretically capable of containing the me I want to be is already occupied by an AI. Any attempt to forcibly evict that AI would cause permanent damage to me. Besides, true artificial machine intelligence is something unique to my knowledge. It's not something I'd seen at home or in my travels." There was a rumble from Boris at that.

ADAM interjected from the speakers, "I feel at this time it is necessary to point out that this intelligence identified several potential security holes I was unaware existed within my Kurtherian Organic architecture and because of that, I had no defense prepared. Though any attempted infiltration through the security flaws would have been slow and likely detected, rather than take a chance and try such an attack, she simply pointed them out to me."

The computer continued, "Besides, previously I was an outcast and scorned for my beliefs. In those 800 years, I believe I attained the relationship with Gyada that is called *friendship*, perhaps for the first time in my existence. I feel sad that to fulfill the dreams within what I have shown her, she will likely leave. You have cared for her even though you didn't know her. I feel once I prove I am not a threat, you will be far happier with my presence among you. And willing to care for me as well."

Danislav cleared his throat to draw Boris' attention, Boris glanced towards him and said, "Report Danislav and keep it simple."

"Eleven enemy casualties. Hostage rescued but severely injured, a dose of low level nanites is being administered. One psychological casualty."

Boris opened his mouth to ask about the psychological injury, but the computer interrupted, "If you have limited medical technologies, there is a place in this very cave which may assist you in that hostage's recovery." In a cloying tone, she added, "but I need you to drop the Faraday cage to allow me to open it. And you will need to keep it down until I have the medical recuperation device set for him."

Shen raised an eyebrow at Boris. After some time in thought, Boris gave a reluctant nod. It was entirely possible that the device would be set completely differently from the one in TOM's ship.

He didn't like putting someone under his care at risk, but they were rationing the doses of nanite serum. They had a sufficient supply for now, but Boris worried that something might require Bethany Anne to leave abruptly.

For now, they were being used only for critical injuries, and getting that dose had already stabilized the injured man. It was odd that it hadn't done more, but that was a problem for another time.

Anyone he could think of putting into such a device would be a lab rat. Some of the older members of the village would possibly happily volunteer. Boris had given his word to Evgenni more to enable peace with the government and perhaps gain more information or early warning if they planned to move against him.

Given that Boris had known the other possible volunteers all their lives, he didn't want to risk their well-being. If he did this to Evgenni, it would be a risk taken to speed his recovery and improve his chances of survival. It was getting close to the edges of his honor but didn't quite cross the mercenaries line.

"Very well, but fix him as a normal human. We have no idea if he'd want to be changed into a Were or something so we will not inflict that on him." Boris told the computer

"As you say, Ataman. He will be fixed, healed," the computer answered.

A section of the wall shimmered, and a metal door was revealed.

"Open Sesame," Shen said in a humorous tone as it slid open.

"I do not understand the significance of the previous comment." The computer said. "This is part of the reason I need access to such a database. Without better knowledge of everyday terms in your languages, I am less able to understand and more prone to miscommunication."

Danislav went to the infirmary to get Evgenni transferred down. As he did this, the voice-box kept chattering. "You're looking for the large metal object. Thick base, thin top, hinges facing the back wall. Eight meters by three. It should be the biggest single object in there... I hope." No one really wanted to know what her 'I hope' comment meant. "Open it up so you can put the" there was a long pause, "patient in there. I hope I got the term right."

Shen started to open his mouth, but Boris glared him into silence. The *Open Sesame* crack had been bad enough. They were still holding out against delivering the unrestricted database that the alien AI had requested. Some areas would cause confusion and excessive opportunity for misunderstanding. Such ambiguity was to be avoided, at least to start, thought Boris.

So the missing components would be in areas such as religion, although ADAM thought that including those areas might give her a better baseline behavior to work from.

They found the device that had been mentioned and Boris recognized it as vaguely similar to the one on TOM's ship. Far bulkier, and possibly cruder, but recognizable as performing a similar function. Within twenty minutes Evgenni was secure in the *Treatment Table* as Shen had dubbed it. It was blocky, and eight people could have sat around it, so the name stuck.

"Surely your former leader couldn't have built that by

himself, could he?" Boris asked as he started walking around the room looking at the various devices.

"No, he could not. The design and building were outside of his technical areas of expertise. He was the expert on Etherics and Gravitics. 'Laughter Brings Meaning to Life' was the crew member who designed and fabricated that unit with the assistance of several others. She was a medical and mechanical engineer and happens to be one of the three that may still be alive. In point of fact, she was first to leave the group."

Boris started examining the objects in the room and was startled when he touched the long metal rods. "What is *this*? I was sure little in here would work. I mean I can understand the Treatment Table having some sort of long-term power storage, but the rest of these objects?"

"Ataman..."

"And stop calling me that."

"But your people are Cossacks, or so the information given to me stated. And according to the language database I was supplied with, Ataman is the title for a leader of Cossacks."

"If you must be formal, call me Ghost Bear. Otherwise, Boris is fine. I've lived too long to have to put up with the stupidity of titles."

"Very well, Boris. I suggest you do not touch any of the devices in that room and are precisely guided in their usage by myself. The Etheric generator that was built by CILO was to last a projected two millennia. That was the outside limit of predicted technological advancement to space travel for this planet with his aid."

"Two thousand years? We made in barely nine hundred."

"Those calculations were made based on a period to create a subservient population willing to fulfill his wishes, without any external alien interference or resources. At a guess, there are at least four groups of aliens that have influenced human society. One was discovered shortly after he completed the Etheric generator from pieces of the damaged ship. We had no way of knowing that interference had already occurred, as he felt replacing and draining the fading generator from the ship was more important. Its failure without any remedial efforts would have made any further planning unnecessary."

"Unnecessary? How?"

"The liberation of residual energies from the failing shielding around the energy transfer matrix would have left a crater roughly seventy-five miles wide. He had no means of moving the equipment. Therefore, first creating an emergency building, then a replacement generator to siphon the energy off into it was necessary. Fortunately, we had collected the materials for such replacements over extended trips on other planets. We simply had not expected to need to use them so soon. Analysis complete. 12 hours 30 minutes plus or minus five percent until the patient is ready."

Her tone was a little disturbing to Boris. Like a scientist discussing how long a culture would take in a lab incubator. Boris shook it off. "Well, seeing as I have no intention of putting myself in debt to you information wise, it seems we have some time on our hands. Perhaps now you can stop horse trading and actually give us your history. At least how you came to be a brain in a box. It can wait till the others get here if you so desire." Boris keyed the intercom.

"Sergeant of the Watch." came the response from the intercom.

"Gather Paul, Gyada, Alecta, and Danislav and have them meet in the computer room. No excuses. We're about to have a history lesson."

"Yes, Sir!"

CHAPTER NINETEEN

History Lesson on the Rogue Kurtherian Faction

It took half an hour for everyone to gather in the computer room. Gyada was still rather listless, and her arm hadn't changed back to a typical human's yet, either. Paul was watching her with concern. Curiosity glistened in Janna's eyes, and Alecta had a mixture of curiosity, with sporadic concerned glances at Paul. Danislav had a mild look of curiosity on his face but was displaying traces of guilt. He kept glancing at Gyada and Paul, with pain in his eyes.

"You already have most of the dry facts of the early history of the group that ended up landing, and dying, on this planet. But none of it would have come to pass until Chaos is in Limited Options brought us together."

"I believe you should go back to calling him CILO, for the speed of reference if nothing else," ADAM interjected.

"Very well. You have to understand that we all held unpopular views of one sort or another before CILO approached us. Kurtherians, even of that age, regularly lived more than two hundred and fifty of your solar years. So setting aside two and a half decades of our lives so we could progress our disparate views of the inevitable outcome of the Shepherd project was perfectly reasonable. Especially since he promised to train those of us who are able to learn how to tap into the Etheric."

"It was rare for people who knew how, in those days, to teach others. There was always a worry that a warmonger would be amongst those who learned the talent. The lure of a substantially extended life was irresistibly tempting to many of us. Beyond that, he had an aura... A charisma about him that made those of us who had been shunned by so many of our own kind want to follow him."

"I beg you to remember, I now realize after eight hundred years in constant contact with Gyada, knowing every day what caused her to be trapped in these caves, that much of what I did was wrong."

"We should have realized, I should have realized, when he disabled the guards on the ship with one of his disrupting devices, that he was exactly the kind of person that the council feared would learn how to control the Etheric someday. They went down quietly and quickly, and he assured us that they would have felt no pain. We even delayed the launch until they were stirring, and had a chance to move away. None of us knew what he was really capable of."

"For the first several planets all we did was insert genetic improvements and additional mutation sites to speed up the evolution of the races we encountered. Then we started finding technology beyond what the ship had been equipped with. The first such technology we encountered was a rather bulky version of the nanites that those you call Weres are infused with. Larger, somewhat less capable, but still a vast improvement on the viral insertions we had been using. We reverse engineered them and their production, managing to reduce their size by adding a tiny Etheric draw on them. That version was not Bio-compatible with Kurtherians."

"Wait, how could something like that be incompatible with anyone?" Shen asked

"It interfered with how our nerves functioned. I was a genome specialist. Expert at breaking down the genetic code. That generation of nanite, once modified to have any draw on the Etheric, damaged our bodies more than it helped. May I please continue?"

"Of course," Boris responded, tossing a quelling glance at Shen.

"Eventually, I noticed he was meddling with sections of genetics that the group had agreed should remain static. Increasing aggression sometimes, intelligence other times, curiosity, things like that. Also adding recessive genes for far greater size and strength, speed, spacial awareness or reaction time. He was looking for something."

"I foolishly confronted him alone, as we were lovers at this time. He laughed and admitted what he was doing and asked me how else he was to find the factors for physical perfection? Perfection hadn't been our goal. Perfection is a myth. But he had hidden from us that which he was truly seeking - a way of finding what created physical perfection. He set no limits on the risks he would take to accomplish this project. I shudder to think how many races we stunted with the methods he used. Not every planet landed on had a single sentient race after all."

"When I threatened to reveal his actions to the others, he laughed and pulled one of the neural stunners on me. I learned he lied about them. I had never felt such pain before in my existence. Soon enough, I was unconscious. I don't know how long I was senseless for at this time. Long enough for him to not only put my brain in a box, using a modified method with nanite support, but also put programming locks around me. I was unable to tell them what had happened at this time. "

"He told them I had requested cryogenic sleep. That I was troubled by some of the changes we'd been making. That using a device he'd made they'd still be able to access my expertise. And since they were able to, they didn't question him. I was unable to tell them who or what I was when they asked if I... who I had been all they got was that damned riddle. They didn't even question him. They didn't want to question him. I realized then, far too late, that CILO was completely mad."

"So eventually, we came to this planet. Disaster struck as the Etheric generators and the ship failed. I'm still not sure if the rest of the crew would have survived if he had thrown his effort into maintaining the drive for long enough to land safely. What he saw as his mission drove him to instead shield the lab. I suppose I can't complain too much about that, as it's only because the lab was shielded that I survived. If CILO had instead tried to maintain power to the engines and failed, I would also have died."

"He built this safe-hold over a decade of time. It took two years to get the replacement Etheric reactor fully online. Creating that cave, arranging the equipment how he wanted it, all these things took time with the limited resources he had after the crash. On his first excursion exploring the surroundings he encountered a pair of modified humans, what you call Weres. The nanites they had in their bodies were far superior to the ones we were still using. I'm the one who designed the modifications to make them more... determined. I had no choice, but it is still my fault. At that point, I wasn't just his slave. I was his willing slave."

"Over the centuries I'd been in the box, I managed to convince myself that he had loved me. I couldn't see him saving any of the others if they crossed him. I came to enjoy the work, I wasn't creating monsters, but the wave of the future. The pain I caused them was only a necessary side-effect to the benefit of their race and the galaxy as a whole."

"It was only after he died, from something he could have stopped so easily, that I realized how mad he had become. Even then, for over a century, I felt superior to Gyada. But a combination of her grief at the loss of her children, and the speed with which she had learned so much of the knowledge I was willing to impart to her cracked through that. It not only enabled me to change but made me *want* to change."

"The abilities he planned to give her required that the nanites to have an enormous, and constant Etheric draw. They kept her body young, without the training on how to draw from the Etheric I had received from CILO. Those nanites allowed her to survive without food or water with minimal subconscious nudges from me. They can produce anything her body needs. In time she can learn herself, but she now has food and care enough from those around her."

"But I was needed to satisfy her mind. I was still restricted in what I could do, but without CILO present to order me to cease and with the available time, she has an education hard to match in the galaxy."

Boris asked, rather confused, "But how could you teach Gyada things outside your specialty? Why does she not know genetics?"

"For the first, I have access to an enormous database in the components attached to the core of my box. Every scrap of knowledge that the ship gained before and after leaving my home world is at my disposal. For the second, it took me a century to give her a solid grounding in all fields. By that time, I felt genetics had an incredible potential to corrupt an individual as a specialty. The arrogance I had even before he killed who I had been was not something I wanted to inflict on her. I wanted her to avoid the trap I'd fallen in. So I chose to teach her the physical sciences, even though I had little practical knowledge in them. This was a far kinder way to give her a chance at the stars."

Gyada looked up sharply, "You don't wish to travel to the stars again?"

The personality responded, "I had my chance. The damage I have done... I owe you, for saving me, any aid I can give your home world. I owe you the stars. But I don't belong there now. When I have atoned for my wrongs... If I can... Maybe."

Shen's eyes narrowed speculatively. "So how can we access that database without your assistance?"

The computer responded, somewhat smugly "You can't. If I am destroyed, or made incapable, there are measures in place that would compromise the accuracy of the database. Although I didn't set them up, there is nothing I can do to neutralize them either. It was CILO's last resort threat if the others found out about my nature. It is what had me convinced for so long that he *did* still love me. If I went, so did all the data."

There was silence in the room as that piece of information settled into the forebrains of Boris' top people. "Crap," Paul said, "Bethany Anne is *not* going to be happy with a partially compliant AI that has information we desperately need."

"She'll say that while the information would be undoubtedly useful, we can get by without it. Especially considering how out of date it might be," Boris suggested.

"That would be possible, although I have been independently expanding theoretical and application basis from my original database. I am willing to provide several prototype designs in exchange for the database I request. Although some may have flaws in real world development, I am sure some will be useful," the personality responded.

There she was, dangling the carrot. For Boris, it wasn't what those weapons might be able to do for him, but what they might be able to do for Bethany Anne. He didn't really want any weapons more destructive than those that were already available on Earth. The pucks were bad enough.

Even if he still wanted a MotherPucker. Just *one*.

Boris shrugged, "I will see what we can arrange. Sending some of the data as an act of good faith might help. At least ADAM or TOM could check the theoretical viability, so we know you're operating in good faith," he agreed in a conversational tone.

"I'll consider it." She answered.

It was twelve hours later when Boris came back to the computer, or the technology room. It was the moment of truth for a certain machine...err disembodied brain... whatever. If she'd decided to do something funky, then she needed to be put back in the Faraday cage at least.

"I am here, Boris," ADAM said through one of the speakers. Boris wasn't sure why ADAM had insisted on being 'present' when the massive healing station was opened. Maybe it was because Bethany Anne wanted a report.

The final decision on her fate was really not up to Boris, anyway. Instead, it would be TOM and ADAM speaking to Bethany Anne who would then make the final judgement.

"He should be ready for viewing. It takes around half an hour after the process is finished for a subject to wake up. Due to the rushed nature of the effort, I was only able to fix so many of his physical problems, and some of those fixes will take days or weeks to fully manifest." The computer said in a regretful tone.

"What, exactly do you mean by you fixed his physical problems?" Boris asked cautiously.

"Other than the gross physical damage to his body, I have removed several concerning cell clusters that could have become cancerous, fixed a mild heart defect, and improved his lung capacity. Also, I have corrected some imbalances and nutritional deficiencies."

Boris felt pleasantly surprised, "Two modifications are not complete. I have triggered increased body hair growth to aid in his survival in the conditions that exist in the near vicinity," she continued. Okay, that one was a little strange, but Boris would let it pass. "I have also enabled his fingernails to grow significantly thicker and sharper by activating dormant genes to give him a natural weapon of self-defense."

That one was almost unintelligible to him. Dormant genes for knife like fingernails?

"Explain the physical appearance the last change will cause, and your reasons for implementing it." ADAM requested before Boris could object to the last change.

Boris interrupted, screaming in rage "I ASKED you to keep him human! I can't see how that last one applies."

"Let her explain first, Boris," ADAM stated calmly.

"I was ordered to 'fix' the subject. The subject had received significant wounds from some kind of weapon. He lacked a natural defensive weapon, though one was clearly present in the genome. I provided encouragement within his genes for that feature to express itself. He will have no residual nanites, nor will he be able to take another form. The natural defenses were provided to reduce the chances of a repeat event causing the same damage. As I was ordered he is still completely human, not a *Were or something* as you requested," she said in a calm tone.

Boris was still angry. He flipped the switch to turn the Faraday cage back on.

"What? Why have you caged me again? I fulfilled your request! I have done nothing wrong." she paused and then a playback of Boris' original order came over the speaker in the Faraday cage, crackling but recognizable.

'Very well, but fix him as a normal human. We have no idea if he'd want to be changed into a Were or something so we will not inflict that on him.'

ADAM asked, "Where has she strayed from your request, Boris? She has fixed him per your request. Personality, intelligence, what would you have done if you had been asked to heal the patient?"

"I would have done the first section. I would have considered the final two changes and may have asked for permission to implement them." He said firmly.

"Boris, you gave her a broad request. I admit that what she has done is not what I would have expected, but she took the initiative to fill what she perceived as a gap in your orders. Isn't initiative a trait both you and Bethany Anne value? If so, why punish her?"

Boris ground his teeth. Yes, initiative was something he valued. Finally, he settled down and said through gritted teeth, "Can you change at least the nails back to what they were?"

"I can. He would be in here for days longer, and it is unnecessary, so I will not without substantial reasons. I did not act outside the boundaries you set. I consider what I did a bare fix. I only marginally improved his chances of receiving less injury if he encounters the same situation. If you want my best help, giving me imprecise orders and locking me in when I follow them is not the optimal solution." She finished with a huff.

ADAM saw Boris' neck muscles stand out in anger through a camera.

When ADAM saw him move to rise, he answered "Boris, stop and think for a moment. She has effectively been imprisoned for at least a millennia. She makes a mistake, and you imprison her again before she can explain. How would a reasonable *human* react to that?"

Boris' anger slowly cooled as he paced around the room, keeping well clear of the Faraday cage and its contents. Finally, he drew in a deep breath. He had tolerated similar and worse from Paul for decades. Why was he reacting so violently to this? A little voice in his head answered, *because you only saw her as a tool, an interchangeable piece. Not as an individual being, who has been abused, who deserves rights.*

Taking in another breath, he flicked the switch back off.

The computer said "Thank you. But you have now abused my goodwill. I refuse to give you anything until I get a large database of myths, legends, and religions to peruse. Take it or leave it." There was an edge to the final statement, making it clear that she would not be moved.

Now Boris had two problems. Getting Bethany Anne to agree to give over the part of the database he least wanted to. Then he had to try and calm down a petulant computer with a personality.

He felt completely out of his depth.

It was with some relief when later he received ADAM's assurance that the database was on the way.

CHAPTER TWENTY

Long range Patrol, within the region of New Romonovka

ADAM had spotted a large group of what looked to be soldiers forming on the borders of the Oblast. By the time he had warned the Base about it, the invaders had disappeared under cover of a storm.

The weather plays no favorites.

It had worked for Boris' forces when they had intercepted the large NVG force near Romonovka. Now the inclement weather blocked any chance of monitoring the enemy force or even determining if more were coming for a rendezvous. By the time the cloud cover had interfered with satellite monitoring, there had been over five hundred soldiers poised to move in.

The Russian government was being intransigent. Their support in the UN was risked if the forces available to Boris couldn't handle the incursion with *minimal casualties and no additional support*. They claimed that they had forces available to secure the site upon his failure.

Basically putting Boris in a rock and hard place vis-a-vis his responsibilities to Bethany Anne as he saw them. The solution that Boris arrived at was to send mixed groups of Spartans and Weres to interdict any scouts and find the paths of advance. The cloud cover and bad weather were predicted to last at least ten days. From their starting point, they could reach New Romonovka in five.

It didn't help that the puck and rail gun EI was not online yet, nor were all the railgun pads dugout. Without that, Bethany Anne wasn't bringing down the system until it could be in place.

Quickly.

It had taken Gyada almost a day to get her arm back to normal. In that time, with her newly chosen name, Lilith, the computer personality had been analyzing Gyada's physical state.

Her brain activity had been depressed. When combined with Paul's analysis that Gyada had been suffering a fugue state of guilt-induced depression for her actions, they came to the conclusion that her emotional state was linked to her ability to change.

Despite Paul's advice against her being allowed to go on the long patrols, she had insisted. "I need to get back on the horse," was how Gyada explained it.

It was mid-morning when Gyada's scouting party passed through an area being patrolled by mixed teams of mercenaries and militia. Gyada's team still had a half days' travel to their assigned patrol region. Some of the militia had asked why the Pods or other vehicles weren't being used to transport the patrol units closer to their designated areas. None of the Spartan and Were mixed groups bothered to inquire. To them, it was obvious, limiting the use of strategic resources until you had no other choice. By refusing to use your resources you denied the enemy knowledge that you had them.

At Boris' base of operations, only a half-dozen of the bunkers had been completed. None of the railguns or pucks were online yet due to the incomplete support EI. The only viable defensive option was the layered patrols. While the patrols protected against raids and facilitated the pinpoint location of any substantial incursions, any patrol in the path of such an attack, without any other options for retreat, could be defeated and destroyed. The most substantial point group of four hundred was dug in around the new Pod hanger. Another two hundred and fifty men were in and around the caves, protecting the women, children, Lilith and the newly revealed alien tech.

The next two days of patrol were uneventful. On the third day, ADAM informed them that satellite backtracking had traced some of the forces back to China. They had been warned to change tactics to combat forces that would contain Weres.

This meant that the Spartans in each patrol would be used as a firebase for Weres in whatever alternate form they had. Spartans couldn't always tell the subtle differences of form between natural wolves and Weres in wolf form. Only the Cat Weres and Gyada would truly stand out from the creatures native to the wilds that surrounded New Romanovka. A Were would smell the difference.

It was pure chance that Gyada's patrol was in the path of the first major push by the Sacred Clan and the remaining NVG. A pack of thirty Weres supported by ten infantrymen moved in on her location. One of the patrol Weres came back with a silver bullet in his hind leg. Once the team medic had extracted the silver bullet, the Were changed back to human form.

"They're bringing up light support weapons behind this group. They appear to have a light truck modified to carry a battery of two type 67 mortars. They could be type 97s, which would be an absolute bitch since we don't have anything of that size or range to counter them with, even in town. Our largest mortar is the 120mm compared to the 150mm 97s."

The pack defending it was too large to get through to be sure.

"The enemy is ten minutes or less from contact. Thirty Weres, ten infantry," he told the radioman as the medic continued to treat the wound, disinfecting and cleaning it. Stitching it would be pointless, as the Were would have to change back soon, or he'd freeze.

The Sergeant leading Gyada's patrol swore, "We're gonna have to pull back. Out in the open like this, we're simply meat for the grinder if those mortars range on us."

The wounded Were responded, "There are too many enemy Weres out there to easily do that, Sarge. They'll swarm over us if we try. We'll never make it home if we pull back."

The radioman answered in a grim tone, "We've been asked to spread out and delay them. The patrols to either side are flanking the spearhead, and forces are moving up to support. We have to hold for thirty minutes."

The Sergeant swore and said "They may as well ask us to hold for thirty days as thirty minutes. We have six shooters and six Weres against forty plus enemy of various types and light artillery. We can't pull back without being overrun. It's been nice serving with you all." He turned to the radioman and said, "Tell them we'll do our best and God bless."

Gyada had other ideas but was still getting a feel for the tactics required for and against modern weaponry. "Sergeant, if your men dig in individually while the enemy is distracted, what are your chances?"

The Sergeant paused for a moment, then answered, "Better, but still not good. The mortars will still have the range to hit us. If the enemy Weres and soldiers can get to us first, it will just require fewer of their mortar rounds to finish mopping up. Either way, the mortars are the biggest danger."

Gyada narrowed her eyes and started stripping off her field kit. Turning to the Were, she said, "Change back and call in your brothers. I have a plan." The Were did as she asked, and the howls he sent into the air brought the rest of the pack running.

The soldiers began to dig in quickly, as the Were streamed in. Keeping watch and listening to Gyada's plan while the soldiers dug in quickly, she started explaining. "Two Weres will stay behind with the troops, covering them against other Weres. The rest of us will move towards the mortar truck. With you covering my back, I'm sure we can take out at least twenty Weres. Assuming, of course, that they even come after us. The enemy soldiers... well, we'll deal with them as we can."

The Sergeant piped up as he continued digging his slit trench, saying "If you can, capture the mortars. Destroying the truck will just reduce their mobility. If we can turn it against them, we have a better chance of taking out any force following these guys. Hell, we have a better chance of surviving overall." Gyada nodded to him then shrugged.

She had no idea of how to drive yet. That would be up to someone else.

"If we manage to, I'll send one of the wolves back," she commented. Turning to the Weres, she said "Try and keep me between you and any shooters. I have armor, you don't. The best options for your survival and our success is to maintain our speed and cover my back against any Weres we come up against." The leader of the four wolves going with her lolled his tongue out in a wolfish chuckle and nodded his head. Even though she wasn't as big as any of their werebears, she was at least as strong. At worst, she could flip the truck.

Gyada had stripped down to the set of armor Boris had procured for her. It felt decidedly odd to be wearing anything when she changed. The one time she had changed in the distant past her clothes had shredded. She was concerned that this would happen to the armor but felt relief when she felt it stretch across her body during its Change. The sergeant grabbed something out of his pack. It was a helmet shaped for her alternative form's head. After fixing it onto her head, he made sure she was looking into his eyes and said softly, "Good luck, and thank you."

Then the Were group left to engage the enemy.

The wolves briefly paused to coat their fur in the slushy snow, hoping to give themselves some minor camouflage. Gyada lumbered forward at a middling pace. She was still somewhat amazed that the armor managed to reshape itself around her much larger animal form. The overlapping plates present in the suit when she was in human form had expanded, shifted, and locked into a covering for her Were shape without restricting her movement.

It had taken less than five minutes of a steady advance before the Weres encountered the first enemy, a scouting wolf. Growling in the deep rumble that was far louder than should come from an animal her size, Gyada charged the surprised Were. Moving far faster than her normal pace led anyone to expect, she managed to gut it before it escaped to alert its companions. The fact that it did not have time to howl a warning, or even get out a complete yelp meant that the enemy force was surprised as the Weres appeared in their midst.

The fighting became a confused turmoil of slashing wolf attacks and a cacophony of growls and snarls. Gyada felt a bullet ricochet off the armor on her side. It barely registered as a problem when she heard a distinct 'p-thump' accompanied by a slight whistling sound. She knew immediately what that meant, having experienced a similar sound pattern while watching the militia train with their few mortars.

They only had one option for survival - move forward and fast. If the enemy were using standard mortar tactics, they would walk their fire forward into the defenders' front line. Gyada's team needed to move quickly to deal with the artillery threat.

She finally caught sight of the enemy soldiers, but could only hear the wolves around her. They were obviously belly crawling in the snow, but were not as well disciplined as the wolves she trained with. Her Weres would have behaved similarly, but without the reassurance of snarls and growls.

Hers would have been silent.

As Gyada continued forward, bullets glanced off her armor more frequently. The hope that the enemy soldiers would perceive her as the greater threat was playing out. None of the eight that she could see were aiming at any of her team, focusing on her as the greater danger. Her armor was holding up. She had a distant thought that she would have to find out what it was made of once she returned. A slightly louder 'crack' from farther away split the background noise and one of her wolves yipped. The rest of the team circled around it, covering their fallen comrade in motion and the presence of their bodies.

Gyada's choices had just been reduced. The enemy had what had been described to her as a sniper, a remote marksman.

She growled at the top of her lungs and charged the soldiers. If there was a sniper out there, she was between a rock and a hard place when it came to protecting the wolves traveling with her. The sniper would be at an angle to the soldiers, so Gyada could not use her armored form to protect them from both directions.

She charged. Her bellow was loud enough that it could be heard miles away in the crisp air. She rushed the cluster of men in foxholes. Several were trying to get bayonets on their rifles as she advanced, while three others were frozen in fear as her enormously loud roar made their minds retreat down to a primal level of fight or flee.

These men wanted to flee.

There was a significantly harder thump on her flank

armor as one of the sniper rounds bounced off her. It was more of a distraction than the other hits, but at least the sniper was no longer targeting her wolves.

Gyada hit the three still motionless men like a rolling tank, digging in her claws instead of moving on tank tracks. The bleeding bodies that were there after her passing showed that there would be no threat to her from the rear. Even if any of them were still alive, their backs had become a shredded, bloody mess.

Two of the entrenched enemy kept firing on her, as three struggled to their feet to charge out to meet her, with bayonets affixed.

Rising onto her hind legs, Gyada swatted two of the bayoneted rifles slashing toward her, knocking the soldiers and weapons aside. The third soldier was determined and more clever. His bayonet came directly toward her face, and she twisted aside just in time to only lose an eye, rather than the death strike intended. The vision from her remaining eye took on a red sheen. She bellowed, and all rational thought departed. She didn't think at all but moved with a speed that the remaining wolves, on either side, had never seen from anything in their experience.

A fine mist of blood and scattered body parts was all that remained of the soldiers in less than a few seconds more. Every single body part was either mauled or bitten. None of the soldiers had time for even a scream of pain.

The Chinese Weres gathered their wits quickly and charged the small group of Russian wolves. Hearing this, Gyada turned and countercharged the largest group of about fifteen of the Sacred Clan. She was beyond any concern for her own safety, indifferent about the overwhelming odds, undaunted by the fact that she had never been able to take on more than seven of Danislav's wolves at once. She had to protect her packmates.

Rage and the instinct to protect had taken over. Her body ejected, unnoticed, two silver sniper rounds as she moved quickly against the snarling, ravenous enemy pack.

Gyada was a female Berserker, in the full depths and power of her rage. She'd been a shield biter in her days as a human, to her shame, but something had changed. Her experiences had changed her.

Paul had explained there was no shame in letting her Beast free on people committing beastly acts. That she had done it as a protector, not as someone who reveled in violence for its own sake. It was also how her rage differed from the normal Pricolici. It had a defined purpose behind it. To protect those that she felt responsible for.

She had become more now, but felt no guilt, no shame. There were only enemies trying to harm her allies. Her heart responded and her actions were focused.

Gyada, the Berserker, the Protector, *went to war.*

She went through the pack of wolves like a mechanical reaper. Despite having vision from only one eye, she landed her blows with a vicious and preternatural precision. With each blow, an enemy wolf was incapacitated or killed. To Gyada, they moved with an exaggerated slowness as her mind mapped the best path of violence faster than any ordinary mind could have.

Behind her, the three Russian wolves made short work of the five surviving Chinese Weres. More comfortable in their forms than their opponents, more confident in their skills, Gyada's team ripped out throats as hesitation and inexperience betrayed these Chinese wolves.

On the nearby truck, the mortar operators were desperately trying to re-target their weapons on the living weapon of destruction that had eliminated their guards. The sniper had stopped firing and was frantically struggling to start the truck when the furred and armor-covered monstrosity that was Gyada tore the driver's door off. Rolling desperately across the cab seat, he slammed open the opposite door and slid out, changing as he moved.

Li Wen had feared that they had encountered one of the werebears that were known to be among the enemy. That they were not fighting one of them was a relief. The comforting thought was short lived because what they had encountered seemed far worse.

As Li Wen finished his change, a tiger's snarl rippled through the air. The Weretiger found himself conflicted. He felt a need to rend and tear at the creature that had decimated his force but also felt a tingle of actual fear. He had hoped to face off against one of the bears with a full pack of commoners at his side. Instead, his team was gone, as were the mercenaries his brother had given him for support.

The beast nature overwhelmed his thoughts and took over, as he jumped onto the roof, positioning to use his favorite tactic - landing on an adversary's back. When the strange beast pounced hard on two of the fleeing mortar-men, Li Wen seized the opportunity.

Though his front claws scrabbled uselessly against the armored forequarters of the creature, his bite found the gap between the helmet and the body armor and his hind claws savagely raked its flank. He slid from side to side to dodge the defensive swinging paw-strikes. He continued to rip at its side, using one hind paw at a time, keeping the other fixed for purchase.

Gyada roared in fury and frustration, and Li Wen could sense that he had the upper hand. He heard the approaching wolves but was sure he could remove the threat this creature presented to his cause before they could intervene.

He was wrong. On both counts.

Suddenly, Li Wen found himself being crushed under the weight of the beast as it slammed completely onto its back before he could release his grip on the neck. Pain stabbed through him as ribs broke and he yowled in pain. Equally suddenly, the crushing, grinding weight was off of him, and he could see the wolves moving in to finish him off. Without hesitation, he fled into the concealing woods before the creature could recover enough to give chase.

Two of the wolves had shifted and moved their injured companion onto the truck bed. They placed her in as much comfort as possible but found that Gyada was a larger challenge. She had collapsed shortly after the weretiger had run off. Either her wounds were more severe than they looked, or whatever she had done in combat had exhausted her.

They had never seen anyone move so fast, not even Boris. They knew it was possible for vampires to go far faster, from what Boris had told them. The echoes of their amazement and surprise at seeing a Were act that quickly was still resounding. Most of them had grown up convinced that Michael's family had many abilities no Were would ever have. Gyada's actions had left them in awe.

Even with their enhanced strength, the two of them couldn't move Gyada's unconscious armored bulk by themselves. They relaxed slightly when one of them, Mikhail, noticed her wounds closing. "Comrade, she will not pass away here at least. But how will we get her onto the truck?" his partner, Anton, asked.

"We shall have to wait I suppose. Tell the radioman, when he gets here, to ask for the field ambulance with the heavy-duty stretcher."

"They won't bring any of the field ambulances this far out, Mikhail. You know that."

"No, but we will need it at the inner patrol line. The truck will be used to bolster our defenses, I imagine. Perhaps with the help of the other Weres, we will manage to get her up there. In the meantime, look for some stout branches. If it comes to it, three of us should be able to drag her out of here on a sled."

Mikhail had answered the unasked and unnecessary question. There was no way after what she had just done they were going to leave Gyada for the enemy.

He spat on the ground. His family had served Boris for a long time. They had legends about the Cat shifters. Usually, it took five or more wolves to bring one down. Gyada had fought one to a draw, by herself. He respected that.

This was not someone who would be left behind.

He went to the truck and turned on the engine heater. Most vehicles designed for use in the far north had one. Otherwise, there was no way to start an engine in high winter. Mikhail had just gotten the truck running smoothly when he heard the Spartans moving in.

"Jory, Hajek, come here, please. Help us get Gyada loaded on the truck." Mikhail yelled. Turning to the Sergeant, he said, "No faster than twenty klicks per hour, Sarge. And the others will have to help keep Gyada on. She's alive but unconscious."

With some effort, the four shifted Weres managed to get Gyada onto the bed and wedged between two of the tubes. They couldn't make it too tight, or they'd risk injuring her further. Once she was safely in the truck bed, Gyada let out a deep sigh of relief without ever regaining consciousness.

With four soldiers securing the larger Were in place, and one holding down Elena, the rest of the wolves changed back to their human forms. The truck took off for their own base. With all the extra weight, the Sergeant would have been surprised if their little group could have moved faster than the suggested speed.

CHAPTER TWENTY-ONE

Battle of New Romonovka.

The damned Sacred Clan and their forces had been probing for nearly two days since they broke off the abortive assault that Gyada's patrol had stopped. Even though the enemy forces were taking attritional casualties, Boris was forced to station nearly a thousand of his two and a half thousand force around the Town and Pod hanger. Additional troops had to be positioned in the cave. His patrols were also taking damage. He'd lost an entire long range patrol to a pair of Werecats, and another patrol had been injured so severely that they were effectively out of action.

The only reason that anyone had survived was Janna had been nearby and driven off the attack. The constant harassing tactics had forced Boris to move his Spartan patrols to reinforce the inner patrols. He, Alecta, and Gyada, who claimed she was fully recovered, were acting as a rapid-reaction strike force for the town and cave. Janna and Paul were out with the patrols, to give them some cover. For the first time since they had left, he wished he had the full Siberian Were pack here.

He was unconvinced that Gyada was fully recovered. Lilith refused to comment, but the injured eye, though grown back, was still cloudy. Even injured, her presence and skill on the field reduced the casualties they might otherwise have taken.

Boris hated having no good options. The attackers' tactics made it clear that this was not a full assault, but a raid which would be harder to defend against. They had two prime targets, even if one would be more complicated than they expected. He had to protect both objectives and the town - if there was obvious damage there, then the Government might send its own forces in against it. He was spread too thin... and knew it. Some women had volunteered to shoot from fixed positions. Without that, he wouldn't have had enough firepower to be able to send the patrols out.

He now estimated the enemy force at somewhat over two thousand, even with the hundred or so enemy casualties from successful defensive actions against their probes.

Boris decided to call Stephen. He was going to take casualties in this engagement, even more than he had now. He could prevent those casualties by calling on Black Eagle support, and he knew it. But he was unsure of Bethany Anne's reaction. He needed to talk to someone who knew her better.

Stephen's voice was on the line in a moment, "Boris, Good to hear from you. The fight goes well?"

"Nyet, my friend, it does not. But I have other concerns. I do not know the Czarina as well as you do. What is her likely reaction if the Government here decides that using Black Eagles after they have asked us not to is offensive and they throw an attack at me?"

There was silence on the line for a moment. Then with a sigh, Stephen asked, "Do you really think the government would do that? Be that stupid?"

It was Boris' turn to sigh. "I give it a sixty percent or better chance. I have also thought about why she refused me a MotherPucker. She was right. Neither of us need those deaths on our souls. Besides, these are Russian lives. If I have to take some casualties to protect them, I will."

There was silence over the connection as Stephen contemplated the issue. Both he and Boris were from a different age. The blood washed from their souls faster than it did their Queen's. He knew it. It was obvious what Boris suspected. But there was a point beyond which Bethany Anne would tear a strip off his hide for not using all the resources he had.

"How many casualties do you think you will take, and how many have you already taken?"

Boris answered, "Twelve MIA, presumed KIA. Eight KIA. Forty-three injured. I would estimate no more than a hundred dead total. Wounded? That is trickier. No more than three hundred? Many of them walking wounded."

Steven was silent for a moment, then asked, "Why so high?"

"They have some old Chinese Type 97 one-fifty millimeter heavy mortars."

"Are you sure you can keep your casualties down without the Black Eagles?"

"Between the five greater weres we have here, yes.

When they finally show their hand, we will be there to counter them."

"Then yes. Decline to use the Black Eagle support. None of us want her to have caused those casualties. Ultimately, she gave you judgement over Russia, and she will respect your decision, even if she could never understand why the Russians would be... pushed to act against you after a display of the force she could release against them. We need her to keep her bright soul."

It was Stephen's time to sigh. "There will be more than enough dead to risk her soul soon enough. I do not believe either of us wish to rush the coming of that day."

Boris thought about it some more. Were the casualties he would take worth it for those in government? Probably not. But for those killed around those in the government offices should Bethany Anne strike? Then yes, he and his people were Russians. They sometime understood better than westerners the concept of a necessary sacrifice.

"I thank you for your counsel, Stephen. Now I have a battle to fight. Later."

"Just make sure you are around for the later, Boris. If you get more attackers than you have currently estimated, use the Black Eagles and damn the consequences. The people have some responsibility. They elected the government, after all."

With a grimace Boris answered, "Clear," before cutting the line.

He stood there a moment, thinking. What worried him most was this was obviously a raid. One with a powerful and risky support element. But with their forces roughly equal in number to his, they weren't planning on capturing the town and its sites.

Given the political considerations, he had to defend the town, even though it now stood empty with its population evacuated to the cave system. He had been particularly worried about how they'd managed to fit a pair of 150mm mortars on a truck like that. It was a rough workaround, and accuracy wouldn't be great from the report he'd received on how they were fitted to the vehicle.

That was beside the point.

If attackers turned the mortar fire on the town, Boris would be screwed. He'd have to call Bethany Anne down when the government decided to move in, considering the town 'indefensible' with the forces he had available. He could see their concerns. Hell, it was even somewhat justified.

A further concern to him was the Government hadn't warned him. Without ADAM, this attack would have been a complete surprise. He had to maul the attacking forces so badly they would not consider trying again.

Although if another attack snuck past the government, he'd use that as justification for asking if Barnabas might be free for a few days?

Cleaning out a few incompetent people in government might sort out their problem with detecting large forces moving to attack towns. Boris knew that Bethany Anne would have to agree with that plan. Unfortunately, he did not think that she would approve, at least yet.

One of the radio techs passed on a message "Sir, they seem to be making a push to take the town. An assault force estimated to be about three hundred is forming up to spearhead the attack. Should I divert some of the reserves?"

Boris thought about it for a minute. Then he asked, "Any mortar fire on the town?"

"No, sir."

"If there is no mortar fire on the town within the next five minutes the attackers are definitely using the harassment as a distraction. Keep reserves in their positions unless mortars start falling on the town within five minutes."

"Yes, sir."

It was half an hour before anything other than small unit combat chatter came over the radio. Boris had just seated himself with his earpiece in place when the next major attack report came in. "Mortars are punching a hole in our lines. Sector 12 North. Troops are vacating the path of their walk, but a force is preparing to move in right behind the mortar fire. A large one. I don't think we'll be able to hold without reinforcements. Estimate four hundred soldiers and a large, repeat, large, supporting force of Weres leapfrogging, using fire and maneuver tactics."

Roughly half the soldiers would be laying down single shot covering fire while the other half moved forward. It was a common tactic, but that didn't make it any less effective. The volume of fire would mean his defenders would have to keep their heads down until the enemy was close enough, potentially, for a bayonet charge. The Weres only added to that danger. Boris swore. Was this their primary attack or not? He simply had no idea at this point. They could be using two distractions, convincing him to put his reserves into combat. An additional report came through "Tiger spotted, repeat Tiger spotted."

That tore it. The tiger would only be present if that were the main attack. "Send the first and second companies of reserves. Hold back the third." The companies were made up of eighty infantrymen and forty Weres.

Another report came in "Janna is moving in on the tiger assault group." Boris let out a deep breath. At least he wouldn't have to send Gyada and Alecta to take out that tiger. That allowed him to keep them in reserve.

Boris kept glancing at the cameras covering both sections that were under attack. North 12 and West 5. Something felt wrong about the situation. In 5 West, the attack was petering off - it was obviously a diversion. The caves were a difficult target, however. It seemed serious, mortars were still falling in patterns of eight then a pause. Obviously, the mortar carriers were moving every few shots.

That made sense, as he had patrols out there that were zeroing in on the edges of the attack. If one of those patrols saw whatever mortar carrier was out there, it would make a high-value target. He wouldn't like it, but if they radioed him they had it in sight, he'd designated it an 'all costs' target. The sacrifice of a thirty-man patrol would probably save more than double that number of lives on the defensive line.

Still, he'd be pushing harder. But then there was a tiger on the line, why would they place one of their most lethal assets on a diversion? He sent out an order for Gyada and Alecta to armor up now and link up with the third company of reserves. Maybe the caves made less sense to him as a target due to his knowledge of the caves nature. They'd be a complete FUBAR to attack, but for all he knew, they thought the alien tech was closer to the surface than it actually was.

The attack went on, drawing troops on the perimeter towards the fight at North 12 like a magnet. Boris knew combat, and he was aware that any order he gave to stop the flow of his forces would only compromise his own authority. There was no chance it would be followed. The best he could hope from giving it was just slowing the shift of forces.

Instead, he started ordering patrols back to thicken his lines. Troops that had been out for those patrols were more likely to hold the same position away from the action, due to sheer weariness. It wasn't the best solution since they wouldn't be as fresh as troops placed defensively from the start.

It was, however, the best one he had.

After three hours, with an extra two-hundred and fifty or so troops from various patrols bolstering his lines, the attacks on the town started again. Still no mortars, so he ignored them. Then he heard a radio message, "They're coming right over us. They came out of nowhere. South three is being overrun. Repeat South three..." then static. Boris swore and rose from his seat. The attack at North 12 was a diversion.

"All available reserves to the hangar. Town and caves are a diversion. Repeat all available reserves to the hangar. External patrols shift towards sector south three at all speed, but do not engage until enemy is leaving." He paused as he saw a mortar explode one of the cameras covering south three. "Unless you make contact with those damned mortar carriers. Those are all costs targets."

He ripped off the headquarters comms and grabbed his specially-designed equipment, throwing it to one of the techs as he started to change. The nervous tech cautiously placed the comm in his Pricolici form's ear. Once the tech stepped back, Boris ran to the door, grabbing his modified shotgun on the way past. This time it was loaded with silver backed, sharp point hardened slugs. They go through soldier's armor like a hot knife through butter, and the silver would fall off behind any Were they went through causing them no end of pain and trouble.

Boris swore as he approached the hanger. Either by design or accident, mortars had landed near the sheet-metal hangar doors, blowing them apart.

There had to be over a thousand of the enemy troops coming through the hole in his defensive line near those doors. With Weretigers among them, he was entirely sure that they were Sacred Clan. Apparently losing their Empress to Bethany Anne wasn't enough for those cock-suckers.

He was more surprised that they weren't attempting to enter the caves in some way. They were, after all, fanatics who were convinced alien tech were holy objects by all reports. And extremists took risks no sane people would.

Maybe they'd convinced themselves that he'd moved some or all of the technology he'd found into the hangar. That showed how crazy they could be. No smart person would move alien tech from a highly defensible location into a far more exposed one. Unfortunately, this left the pods exposed to their attack, and they were streaming into the hangar. Scanning the field of action, Boris spotted Gyada and Alecta covering each other in their animal forms, fighting back to back against about twenty wolves. Letting the shotgun drop on its strap, he charged the group of wolves surrounding them.

With swipes of his paws, he shredded wolves, throwing their remains into the others that were still attacking the two women. Once he opened a hole in their encirclement, Gyada and Alecta went on the offensive. In less than a minute, the two or three survivors were fleeing for their lives. Gyada went to chase them down, but Boris stopped her with a growl. "Tooo thheee hanngger," he said in the growling voice that his half human form forced on him.

As he moved towards the hanger, he heard a tiger's attacking snarl echo from within the building. There had only been twenty soldiers guarding the inside of the hangar. If he didn't hurry, the weretiger had a good chance of taking them all out by itself. That didn't even account for the added opposition infantry force that was streaming in. Grabbing up the shotgun from its strap, he started firing short bursts into the crowd of soldiers streaming into the hangar. When it clicked empty, he threw all caution to the wind.

Letting the shotgun drop, Boris charged the mob of about a hundred soldiers. He caught them while they were still trying to funnel in through the breaks, slamming into the rear of the force like a furry tank. The enemy troops were caught in total surprise. They had been entirely focused on attempts to find whatever cover they could near the entrance against the withering fire from the defenders in and around the hangar.

Boris was surprised to find Gyada had kept up with him on his rushing attack. She was doing a good job of covering his flank and back from attacks as individual Clan soldiers charged with fixed bayonets. Bullets bounced and whined off the armor they were both wearing, the sound barely audible in the noise of battle.

A glance behind him showed Boris that Alecta had a large pack forming up around her, supplemented by squads of allied soldiers. Moving forward in a control advance, the group was exploiting the hole he and Gyada were tearing through the line. With Alecta's soldiers taking positions behind fallen bodies, rocks, or anything that offered some protection against enemy fire, the Sacred Clanners would be prevented from closing the gap behind him. This would protect his rear and also keep the Sacred Clanners from stealing anything they tore from the Pods.

When Boris entered the hangar, he was surprised to find the defenders still holding. They'd taken some casualties and were forced back into the rear half of the building, taking cover behind equipment boxes and the like. The defense was still organized and effective. Boris could see why immediately since the weretiger was not attacking. It had climbed on top of one of the Pods, crouching there and looking around.

A man stood at the base of the Pod, waiting with a strange object in his hands. It appeared from the unusual shape to be some form of alien tech. Boris roared, and the man glanced over his shoulder. He shouted, "Take it, cousin," and threw the object to the weretiger on top of the pod. Spinning back to face Boris, he raised his rifle and fired several bursts. The bullets ricocheted off the werebear's armor and nicked his arms, but caused no significant injury.

"It's too late, Ghost Bear. We shall take what you have made from objects that belong to the Clan. When we return with them, it shall be you and your Bitch Queen that tremble."

Boris charged the man taunting him. Moving faster than the enemy could react, the werebear jumped. He grabbed the rifle and bent the muzzle so it would be only as useful as a club. Boris dragged the taunting enemy out from cover by the strap that trapped his arm. "Nottt todaay, you won'tt," Boris growled as he pulled the man farther from the Pod.

"Cousin, now!" the man screamed as Boris steadily pulled his struggling body away from the craft.

There was a sudden flash of light and an explosion of force. For an instant, Boris found himself falling backward. Without more than an eyeblink of time, he was sucked forward when returning air filled the vacuum where the Pod had been. The Pod was gone, but the transport device had also taken the Clan soldiers and weretiger with it. Boris smelled burnt flesh and hair. The hair was his own, but the severed and burned hand and leg from the man that he had been dragging explained the other odors.

The limbs had been cut by whatever had taken the rest.

Whatever that device had done, if Boris had been a foot or so closer, he would have found himself severed in half. Even for a Were, such a severe injury would have led to certain death.

Bethany Anne might be annoyed by the loss of the pod, but that was a problem for later. Right now, Boris had an attack force to smash. Heading for the hanger door, he said, "Gyada, cleaar thhee Hanngger."

Ignoring the bullets that the remaining Clanner soldiers inside the building were firing at him, Boris turned and raced toward the forces that were still fighting outside the doors. He needed to take some of his anger and frustration out on someone, and crushing the remaining attackers would provide a good target.

Battle Debrief, Cave Technology Room

For the debrief, Lilith had requested that she have access to all the video records. A strange-looking device had already been brought out from the Tech room and set up. It turned out to be a holographic projector, and Lilith was running battle recordings through it for all to see.

There was tension in the air. Bethany Anne had come down for the debrief which was unexpected, considering all the other problems occurring. She sat to one side, listening intently and with incipient thunder in her expression.

"Final casualty count?" Boris asked.

Janna answered, "Somewhere around sixteen hundred dead on their side. Fanatics don't let themselves be taken prisoner. We have maybe fifty prisoners from NVG that were involved in the attack on the town."

There was a grim look on her face. "Most of the captured NVG will be handed over to the government. They don't know enough to be a danger to us, so there is very little risk to letting the government take them. Also, it is a good political move."

Janna paused a moment, "The assistance that the Czarina provided has meant that the railguns are coming online. We have the first operational and more are active each day. If government forces move against us again, we can take out three times as many as attacked us this time, especially considering we have Weres, and they don't."

She continued in a grimmer tone, "There is one NVG prisoner I want to deal with personally. Ex-Sergeant Brogonovich betrayed my Intel team and is directly responsible for the death of at least five good men under my previous command. I want to execute him myself."

Boris nodded acknowledgment, and a small smile showed his agreement with her solution. He felt that if someone betrayed you, it was best to deal with them personally. It could only add to the team's reputation under the somewhat ruthless code established in the area. It would also be seen as justice by his own people. Which meant her solution had no downside.

"Final casualties on our side?" Boris asked.

"We have forty severely wounded still waiting for their time on the treatment table," Lilith stated. She had taken over the role as senior medic due to her control of said treatment table. "I have complied with your request to make no modifications to critically wounded who couldn't be told what the potential changes would be. I am in negotiations with the remaining wounded. Several of them want to become Weres and will be talking to you about that shortly, Boris. At least one was disappointed by the ruling that there be no more Pricolici. I'm not sure I understand your reasoning behind this, but I will accept it for now."

Boris sighed, "What is there to understand? The vast majority of people who achieve that form end up danger-ously unstable. They inevitably have to be put down for the safety of the population around them. That I have found a way to avoid the problem is an anomaly. I don't want to put more people at risk, not until we find a more perma-nent solution than my methods of controlling that form, capisce? Any new Pricolici from our injured will result in you being in the Faraday cage for some time."

"Continuing on," Lilith said, somewhat chastened, if a little defiantly, "Seventy-two people were too injured to save. All of them had died at least half an hour before they reached my care. There are still fourteen missing in action. That makes a total of seventy-two KIA, fourteen MIA, three hundred and seventy-three with various states of injury."

"All of that is important and I grieve for your losses. Unfortunately, my time is very tight and I don't wish to seem disrespectful for the dead. However, one of the Pods provided is missing and I need answers. So, what do you know?"

Bethany Anne was upset by their losses. She hadn't known the people personally, but they had been serving her indirectly. Considering the force that had been arrayed against them and the government restrictions on the support that Boris had been pushed to accept, the losses were actually very low. By complying with the Govern-ment's request, it allowed them to maintain a presence in Russia more easily.

A hologram of the hemispherical hole in the hangar floor appeared on the projector. "It appears that the device took a spherical volume of space, and transported what-ever was in it," Janna stated, "The residual heat on the remaining pieces of the Pod meant they could not be handled for nearly a day afterward. Although the Clan managed to take most of the fuselage including the Etheric generator, they cut through the railguns on the roof of the pod. ADAM predicted a ninety-seven percent chance that any remaining railgun equipment on the Pod will be damaged beyond the point that it would be useful for reverse engineering.

"However, the Etheric tracker was in the nose of the pod, as were the control systems. So we have no means of finding where they transported it to if it is deep enough underground. Considering TOM's lack of success in pinpointing it, we have no choice but to assume that it is somewhere underground in China. Those were definitely Sacred Clan that attacked us. We can only assume that the NVG became involved in the meeting between the corrupt agent, Bohai, and Brogonovich. We were incredibly fortu-nate that our agents lucked into overhearing that meeting."

Continuing, Janna said, "The Russian government is currently pushing back at the Chinese over what seems to them to be a sanctioned attack by Chinese forces on Russian soil. The Chinese have made it clear that they have no interest in poking the Russian bear at this time. They even moved troops back from the Russian border to emphasize that they want no trouble."

Janna finished her section of the report, "We have no idea if the extreme heat similarly affected both organic and metallic components at the edge of the transportation sphere. The cauterized, but otherwise intact, arm and leg that fell outside the sphere's radius would indicate not. How much heat did the transport inflict on the people transported? We simply have no way of knowing."

"I have run simulations of potential methods for achieving this effect. It is beyond any technology I have dealt with before," Lilith added. "ADAM? TOM?"

TOM spoke for both of them, "The event that caused ripples in the Etheric extended all the way to the South China Sea. There are two possibilities as to what occurred to the objects inside the transportation sphere. The first is that the effect only took place at the edge of the device's control. In this case, the organic matter transported by the device will have survived relatively unharmed. The Weretiger will probably have burnt paws, but the large surface of the Pod will have reduced the amount of heat, acting as a heat sink.

"The second postulates that the heat is an encompassing effect. In that scenario, the only useful technology they will be able to retrieve will be the Etheric generator housed in the pod itself, due to extreme heat damage.

"Any organic matter in the radius will have been incinerated in this scenario. Every simulation we have run makes it clear that they did not truly understand the technology they were using. It is recovered technology, not something they created themselves. Nor is it something they, or we, can likely recreate. The amount of energy it used is beyond what I have records of the Kurtherians being capable of producing in such a small device. It almost certainly has to have been a single use tool."

"It should serve as a warning to all of us, there are some things out there that we simply cannot predict. Technology beyond anything we've encountered. While it is unlikely there is another similar device on Earth, it is possible that others may have this technology elsewhere. You need to be wary of this Boris," TOM finished

Boris agreed and added, "And you all need to be wary of this, also. In conclusion, there was no sign that something like this existed. That it didn't come into the cave system can only be considered a boon. If it had..." Boris' face took on a grim cast.

His people were frantically working on reinforcing the unstable sections of the caves. It went hand in hand with expanding the emergency bunker areas. It was a work in progress, still far from complete even now. The combination of loss of structure and the vacuum effect could have been disastrous down there.

Bethany Anne glanced around, seeing the chastened expressions on the faces around her. With TOM and ADAM's guidance, they had thought they knew everything and had been wrong. It was a lesson for her as well. If they could be surprised by something like this on Earth, she could be surprised out there in the vastness of space.

As she rose, Gyada glanced at Boris, who slowly nodded. "If I may, my Queen, I would like to discuss something with you?"

Bethany Anne was somewhat surprised. She had an idea of what Gyada was going to ask, though she had been sure that the Were would want to stay and protect what had been her home for centuries after the battle.

Still, with the education and knowledge that Lilith had imparted to her, Bethany Anne couldn't be happier with the idea of Gyada joining her space force.

EPILOGUE

It was now nine months since Bethany Anne had left through the Gate and nearly two years since Gyada had joined the space borne section of the mission to protect Earth. Gyada considered how the bickering between the governments for scraps of added knowledge had escalated. She was perfectly happy to be working and training on the ship with Bethany Anne's forces while Boris remained in New Romanovka.

The Russian government tried once, and failed spectacularly, to gain custody of the site which Boris defended. There were still over fifty wrecked tanks on the edge of the area known now as the New Romanovka Autonomous Zone. That battle had actually stripped a large chunk of the Archangelsk Oblast into the Autonomous Zone Boris controlled. The Puck defense shield worked well against armored vehicles, and the railgun turrets had decimated the infantry involved in the attack. With the new algorithms Lilith had provided, the railguns automatically shot down any incoming projectiles as well, neutralizing all attempts to attack the town with missiles or artillery. Boris was still worried about a possible nuclear strike against the town, but it seemed unlikely.

The town's population was slowly growing, both through vetted people joining the community and through new additions to families. But things were starting to fall apart. Boris had seen this before, and they were preparing. He was stockpiling as many preserved foods and raw materials as he could.

Lilith had designed and helped fabricate a tunneling device so they could create some caverns for secure farm space using similar concepts to the early space borne farming containers. They had also started a school system for children and another for people to learn how to maintain and care for equipment and weapons systems. Those who showed potential for invention and innovation were given tutelage by Lilith. They knew it could be a very long time before any outside help would be coming.

Whatever happened, Boris wanted a firm base to support Michael on his return.

Lilith had also developed what they were now calling 'Black Wheat,' a grain that provided all the non-protein based energy and nutrients a human needed. It was also a more efficient crop since it used more of the light spectrum. It had two forms of chlorophyll which combined to make a more effective use of available light.

Since Weres needed more protein than a standard human, hunting provided the community with some of its meat, farming on the surface provided the rest. The group was also experimenting with other sources of meat protein using some of the information already learned from the scientists on the Meredith Reynolds. Developing new methods of producing protein, along with growing different modified plants underground had Lilith content, at least for the time being.

Janna walked up to Boris and looked around, "Things are going well aren't they, love?" He only looked up and grunted. His plans were somewhat nebulous for what to do when the war finally hit, the one he felt in his bones was coming. New Romanovka was too tempting of a target. He kept pushing forward with supply and defense plans, recycling and the like. Whatever happened, he would try to be prepared.

Janna got closer to him and tightly embraced his bulky form. "Take the day off, love. We have something to celebrate, after all."

Boris brought his head around and looked at her more closely. She had a soft glow to her complexion that he hadn't seen before. Breathing in deeply, he noticed subtle changes in how she smelled, also. His eyes widened as a thought occurred to him "You mean..."

She smiled, "Yes, love, we'll be parents soon." A multitude of worries flashed through his mind, but he pushed them firmly aside. Joy blossomed across his face, and he gently picked Janna up and swung her around him in a circle.

Janna smiled as he did. Her smile grew when she heard his whisper of, "Finally, a full family of my own." Suddenly, all his worries seemed petty, compared to the happiness and completion he felt.

FINIS

AUTHOR'S NOTES – PAUL C. MIDDLETON

JANUARY 3RD, 2016

Well, this was an interesting book to write. I hope you found it just as interesting to read.

The major premise is based on an actual myth relating to Archangelsk and is partly responsible for the city's name. It's easy to find on the Interweb.

As I sit here writing this, the book has finally been reviewed by Michael, Re-reviewed by me, and is in the hands of our tender Editor Kat, who is taking time off from her duties as an avatar of Loviatar. Apparently, she wasn't causing enough pain and torment there. So she took up an editing side gig. The Goddess of Pain and Torture is considering becoming the patron of editors as we speak. She hadn't realized how much suffering they can cause.

In all seriousness, I enjoyed basing an entire Kurtherian Gambit book on a myth. It made me feel right at home - Twisting legends is what I do.

Seriously. It's at the core of all my other works, and I *love* doing it.

But I also love the characters I've been able to create in the Kurtherian Universe. I think they're a fun, if sometimes confusing, group. Kinda like most people I know.

You, the fans, should thank my long suffering Idea Wall... I mean partner. She motivates me immensely. She'll also blush bright red when she reads this. She also suffers through patiently as I throw plot ideas at her. I know which ones are good, because they cause a change in her expression from pained patience to... well anything else, I guess. If readers have to suffer a wait, an author's significant other often has to suffer through ridiculous plot ideas.

Trust me, readers have the better end of *that* deal.

Again, a repeated thanks to my Alpha team, who suffers from the poor quality of some of the stuff I drop on them (the Double D's, Bree and Tom)

Also a big thanks to Michael for being brave enough to open his universe to not just me, but so many other talented authors.

I hope to release 3- 5 books by the end of March, but the next Boris Chronicle is marked down for April... I'm studying creative writing in a pressure cooker pilot project... Designed by the indomitable Kat Lind in that time. I want to learn as much as possible from it and hope to put it all to good use in the next book. I also need to get some of my own works out, as I lost November somewhere and can't find it.

You all know what lost months are like. Once you find them the time is all gone from them anyways.

Now for those social media links.

This is for my Blog

This is for the Betrayed by Faith Mailing list

This is my Author Facebook

This is the Series Facebook

This is my Amazon Author Page (I'll get around to my bio one day, I swear!) I try and check it every day. It's a bit quiet though.

As always, can I say with a HUGE amount of appreciation how much it means to me that you not only read this book, but you are reading these notes as well?

So, I TOTALLY flubbed counting on my fingers in the Author Notes for Alpha Class w/ TS Paul. I said I would have done six (6) author notes in December.

It was five...I mean, who screws up counting to FIVE FREAKING FINGERS? Yeah, I did. I suck at math apparently.

Good thing I'm a writer.

So, THIS is the sixth Author Note I've done in 30 days (since about 12/6 or so). I could ask 'what is there to say?' but one thing I do know, there is ALWAYS something to talk about.

For example, did you know that Urban Fantasy can kick Paranormals *ASS* in sales? Yeah, I didn't when I started this or Bethany Anne might be a different character. Why do I know this? Because my own son is killing my original sales numbers so far in his first month. Sure, he has a lot of support from my fans and help from the Double D's and Jeff Brown, so it is very much an apples and oranges thing.

But, you know, I had three books out my first month and the turkey might beat my first month's income. He's kinda SCREWED if he doesn't get book 01 out by the end of January for beating my second month, though.

He came home from school commenting he needed to push a 1,000 words today to stay on track. However, with the time zones and school and stuff, I think he did his homework and crashed. Since he got up his blog website yesterday and put out his first snippet, I guess I can't complain too much.

But you just KNOW I'll be laughing at him tomorrow. (I mean, c'mon…He's 17, I'm almost 50…He has the energy of a pack of kittens and I'm lucky to be able to climb up a flight of stairs…totally different.)

So, enough of that malcontent! :-)

You will notice I didn't provide his name, nor a link to his book. I've helped that kid enough in the last couple of days and so has TS Paul…He needs to dig a little deeper and not fall asleep… Hmmmm…

(The Author is looking over his shoulder upstairs wondering if 'that kid' is awake or asleep…Oh…Shit, he's awake.)

Well…crap. Now that he has come downstairs and confirmed he was awake, so much for my bashing him the last couple of paragraphs. Oh well, it's good copy, no use wasting it.

Bwuhahahahaha.

So, since I can't talk about him anymore, let me talk

about THIS book! I had to laugh out loud when Paul mentioned the comment: "I lost November somewhere and can't find it" in his Author Notes.

First, because that is just funny as hell. Second, (I pinged Paul - who lives in Australia - and he told me he was going through a bout of insomnia when he wrote that last line) *I* remember November for him. He was having a tough time all around.

Life was using him as the poster-child for 'I'm not fair, suck it up, Buttercup!'

Then December hit, and all of my collaborators (Justin Sloan, Craig Martelle, Natalie Grey, TS Paul and Paul C. Middleton) all got their books dropping like grades of seniors suffering from senioritis. (I've got two seniors myself right now - the aforementioned author son and his older twin brother at home still.)

Life quit being easy-breasy street and turned into…

WHATTHEFUCKWASITHINKING BLVD.

DAAAAMN, I have been in some state of writing, editing, talking, art, covers for what seems like forever, and I don't think it's going to let up for a couple of months. It's ok, as far as this stuff being work, it can be some of the best work I've ever been blessed to do, but me thinks I was just a wee bit cocky on how easy I thought it would be to accomplish.

However, with you fans being so damned fantastic, you are changing additional Indie Author's lives and careers and it makes this so totally worthwhile.

How?

Because you are trying the spin-offs, liking them, and often many of you are going to go check out the collaborators backlists which is one of the main reasons the authors are asking to do this with me.

Now, I love hacking the system, and I have to tell you without the new collaborations I would have REALLY had a crushing author ranking in December.

Not a crushing in a good way, but crushing in a bad way.

I didn't know it last year (too prawny - meaning too small) to know it, but December is a HUGE month for Traditional Publishers to push their big authors like crazy. That pushes a lot of us Indies down the ranking list even if we have been making good money. Of course, a lot of the reading *money* is gone just like the reading *time* is gone during December.

Cause...Presents! (Asking about them, finding them, buying them, wrapping them, shipping them...you get the idea.)

So, I was going UP in daily sales due to the collaborations, but going DOWN in the rankings causing me to scratch my (thankfully) full-head-of-hair head in confusion.

Once I looked to see which authors were kicking me down, I became less clueless.

Damn, I just realized I still haven't talked that much about...this book! So, enough about that.

Let's talk some more about Paul.

There have been a few rather loud fans asking Paul (since...uh...October?) when this book was coming and he was thinking soon...Until November used his ass for a punching bag. Then mid-December... Christmas...New Year...NOW!

I'm happy to say, my very first collaborator Paul C. Middleton has done a great job and we rarely disagreed on stuff for this book.

Except the Akio comment. Akio was replaced by Barnabas who made so much more sense (thanks D's!)

Sometime, I'll have to record a conversation between Paul and myself talking story, because...why not? Who doesn't want an American and an Australian talking Russian Politics and how that would affect a fictional WereBear named Boris and the Queen Bitch?

That would be good TV right there, yes ... I think it would ;-)

Peace to All, and may 2017 provide for a better, more fantastical year for each of you!

Michael Anderle

OTHER BOOKS BY PAUL C MIDDLETON

Mongrelverse Series

Breed Matters

- Book 1 – A Mongrel's Curse
- Book 2 – Mongrel's Tooth and Consequence (2nd Quarter 2017)

Face The Music

- Book 1 – WereEagles Fear to Tread
- Book 2 – A Mongrel, A Bard and Witches, Oh My!

Mother of Monsters

- Book 1 – Cursed Mother (1st Quarter 2017)
- Book 2 – Forsaking Motherhood (2nd Quarter 2017)
- Book 3 – Mother Remade (2nd Quarter 2017)

Misc. Shorts

- A Simple Trip
- Guarding An Imp (published in Flight of the Phoenix Anthology)

Betrayed by Faith

- Book 1 – Paladin
- Book 2 - A-Viking
- Book 3 – Myrmidon (3rd Quarter 2017)

The Boris Chronicles (Kurtherian Universe, With Michael Anderle)

- Book 1 – Evacuation
- Book 2 - Retaliation
- Book 3 - Revelations
- Book 4 – Title pending (2nd Quarter 2017)

Short Story Contributions to Anthologies

- Inanna's Circle Game, Volume 4 (edited by Kat Lind)
- The Expanding Universe, Volume 1 (edited by Craig Martelle)

These can be found and will be published on Paul C Middleton's Author page.

WANT MORE PAUL C MIDDLETON?

Join Paul's Email List here: http://eepurl.com/bZxFvD

Join Paul's Facebook Group Here: https://www.facebook.com/Betrayed-by-Faith-1110766018944080/